A BOOK OF
MODERN STORIES

Edited by
HESTER BURTON

Illustrated by
JOHN W. LAWRENCE

OXFORD UNIVERSITY PRESS

Oxford University Press, Ely House, London W.1

GLASGOW NEW YORK TORONTO MELBOURNE WELLINGTON
CAPE TOWN IBADAN NAIROBI DAR ES SALAAM LUSAKA ADDIS ABABA
DELHI BOMBAY CALCUTTA MADRAS KARACHI LAHORE DACCA
KUALA LUMPUR SINGAPORE HONG KONG TOKYO

First published 1959
Reprinted 1962, 1963, 1964, 1972

Printed in Great Britain by Richard Clay (The Chaucer Press), Ltd.,
Bungay, Suffolk

INTRODUCTION

STORY-TELLERS do not sit in an empty market-place. Their trade is to keep their audience spellbound at their feet; if the crowd fidgets and moves away, they have failed. Yet even the most sensational and eloquent of story-tellers has not succeeded in his art if his hearers return home no wiser or kinder than they set out. A good short story not only holds our attention but also stretches our imagination, enlarges our sympathies and widens our understanding of the world in which we live.

The short stories in this selection have been chosen because the editor hopes that they will give pleasure to boys and girls in their early and middle teens. She hopes, too, that they will give their readers those deeper and more lasting gifts of the story-teller's art.

Now that the highest mountain in the world has been climbed and the lowest depth in the Pacific plumbed and that most of us live lives very like those of our neighbours, there is a great need for us to stretch our imagination in our reading. If 'there is nothing left remarkable beneath the visiting moon', then we must go beyond it. Science fiction and space fiction provide this generation with that sense of the marvellous which travellers' tales gave to the Elizabethans. Desdemona listened spellbound to Othello's stories of cannibals and

> The Anthropophagi, and men whose heads
> Do grow beneath their shoulders.

It is hoped that Ray Bradbury's two stories in this selection will enthral modern boys and girls in the same way.

One brings the prehistoric past into the present; the other projects us forward in time and space. Both, by the vigour and poetry of their style, stir the imagination.

When Othello had finished his narration, Desdemona gave him for his pains a world of sighs.

> She swore,—in faith, 'twas strange, 'twas passing
>   strange,
> 'Twas pitiful, 'twas wondrous pitiful.

She had lived Othello's griefs and dangers with him as she listened. Every good tale should make its hearers feel the joys and griefs of its characters within their own hearts. This experience enlarges their awareness of other human beings. When we are old hands at reading we can come to sympathize in this way even with murderers and saints and prigs. But when we are less experienced in these voyages of understanding, we must stray less far from home. The heroes and heroines of the stories in this selection are neither criminals nor paragons of virtue. They are mostly very ordinary decent sorts of people, knowing the same temptations and hopes and fears as ourselves, and overcoming their difficulties with the kind of courage that most of us can summon to our aid in moments of extreme crisis. It is not impossible that the young wives in *Fear* and *A Mild Attack of Locusts*, the young man in *The Half-Mile* and the two children in *The Man of the House* and *My White Donkey* could be ourselves.

Lastly a good short story not only teaches us more about our fellow creatures and, consequently, about ourselves; it also widens our knowledge of the physical universe in which we live. These stories come from many parts of the English-speaking world. Two describe life in Ireland; one comes from Africa, two from Australia, one from New

Zealand; one is a credible account of Mars. Two of the writers, Katherine Mansfield and Liam O'Flaherty, wrote the stories which appear in this volume with all the passionate longing of people exiled from their native land. 'Ah the people—the people we loved there!' wrote Katherine Mansfield about New Zealand, 'Oh, I want for one moment to make our undiscovered country leap into the eyes of the Old World.' * Liam O'Flaherty, depressed and starving, was walking the streets of London, when he suddenly thought—'How beautiful to stand on a cliff in Aran! . . . This joy found words . . . It seemed as if a dam had burst somewhere in my soul, for the words poured forth in a torrent." † It is out of emotions such as these that writers can make countries 'suddenly leap into the eyes' of readers who, by reasons of poverty or chance, may never have an opportunity of travelling beyond their native shores.

---

* From *Journal of Katherine Mansfield* edited by J. Middleton Murry.
† From *Shame the Devil* an Autobiography by Liam O'Flaherty.

NOTE

THE SHORT introductions to some of the individual stories are intended to help readers to understand at the outset the background of the stories which they are about to read. The short biographical notes on some of the authors (to be found at the end of the volume) have a two-fold purpose. First, they suggest how each writer may have come to write the story which appears here; and secondly, they give the titles of other books written by the same author which may appeal to readers.

ACKNOWLEDGEMENTS

THE EDITOR wishes to thank the following authors and publishers for permission to reprint these copyright stories:

Mr T. O. Beachcroft and The Bodley Head, for *The Half-Mile* from *A Young Man in a Hurry* and *My White Donkey* from *Goodbye Aunt Hesther*; Mrs Lessing and Messrs Macgibbon and Kee for *A Mild Attack of Locusts* from *The Habit of Loving*; Mr Ray Bradbury and Messrs Rupert Hart-Davis Ltd., for *The Fog Horn* from *The Golden Apples of the Sun* and the two extracts *The Settlers* and *The Green Morning* from *The Silver Locusts*; Mrs Mitchison and Messrs Jonathan Cape Ltd., for *The Hostages*; Mr E. Schlunke and Messrs Angus and Robertson Ltd., for *The Enthusiastic Prisoner* from *The Man in the Silo*; The Society of Authors, as literary representatives for the late Miss Katherine Mansfield, for *Her First Ball*; Mr Frank O'Connor and Messrs Macmillan and Co. Ltd., for *The Man of the House* from *Traveller's Samples*; Mrs H. Drake-Brockman and Messrs Angus and Robertson Ltd., for *Fear* from *Sydney or the Bush*; Mr Liam O'Flaherty and Messrs Jonathan Cape Ltd., for *Trapped* from *The Short Stories of Liam O'Flaherty*; Mr Richard Hughes and Messrs Chatto and Windus Ltd., for *A Night at a Cottage* from *A Moment in Time*.

The Editor is also most grateful to the following authors for information about the composition and background of their stories: Mr T. O. Beachcroft, Mrs Lessing, Mrs Mitchison, and Mrs H. Drake-Brockman.

CONTENTS

THE HALF-MILE
By T. O. Beachcroft   11

A MILD ATTACK OF LOCUSTS
By Doris Lessing   28

THE FOG HORN
By Ray Bradbury   40

THE HOSTAGES
By Naomi Mitchison   53

THE ENTHUSIASTIC PRISONER
By E. Schlunke   67

HER FIRST BALL
By Katherine Mansfield   78

THE MAN OF THE HOUSE
By Frank O'Connor   89

THE SETTLERS. THE GREEN MORNING
By Ray Bradbury   102

FEAR
By H. Drake-Brockman   111

TRAPPED
By Liam O'Flaherty   123

MY WHITE DONKEY
By T. O. Beachcroft   135

A NIGHT AT A COTTAGE
By Richard Hughes   150

BIOGRAPHICAL NOTES   154

THE HALF-MILE

This story from the running track was written over thirty years ago. In those far off days the record time for the half-mile was 1 minute 52 seconds. The social distinctions were different, too. At provincial athletic meetings, such as the one described here, visiting athletes from Oxford and Cambridge were expected to win most of the races.

Thirty years of running have knocked sixteen seconds off the record time for the mile, but it has not dimmed the courage of Andrew Williamson's first 'class race'.

There is a timelessness about the discipline of the running track; the Greek runners in the Olympic Games knew its rigours twenty-five centuries ago, and in a future generation the first runner to complete the mile in three minutes will know it too.

The hero of this story, a skilled craftsman in a pottery works, knew the truth of this ageless triumph.

'After all, running is a thing man has always done . . . a good runner is a good runner for all time—with hundreds and hundreds of years of kinship behind him.'

SATURDAY NOON. The town hall clock boomed the hour in the distance. All over the town, hooters called to each other from street to street. From the gates of twenty different potteries men, women, boys and girls streamed. Ones and twos grew to a steady flow, then died away again to ones and twos.

Andrew Williamson, a dipper at the Royal Chorley, was stopped at the gate by old Jones the doorkeeper.

'So long, Andrew,' he said, 'good luck for the half-mile.'

Andrew glanced at him, and looked away self-consciously.

'How did you know I was running?'

'Oh, I takes an interest,' said Joe, 'used to run a half-mile myself.'

'Go on?' said Andrew. 'I never knew.'

'I was good for one-fifty-eight,' said the old man. 'That was good going in those days.'

'Go on?' said Andrew again. 'But that's class running. That's a class half-mile.'

'Oh, I dunno, plenty on 'em do it now!'

'Well, I wish I could. That's my ambition: to get inside two minutes. I've never beaten two-four yet!'

'Well, this is just the day for it,' the veteran told him. 'You have a nice trot round first: get some good summer air into your lungs: you'll win.'

'But I've never run in a class race,' Andrew persisted. 'I've only done Club races. I can't hope for more'n a place; look who's running.'

'Who?' said Jones.

'Well, there's six of us in the final. Let's see: Joe Brewster, the cross-country man; he can run a four-thirty mile, and now he wants to try the half.'

'Well, he'll never do two minutes,' said Jones, 'take it from me.'

'Then there's Perry, him as ran at the "Three Clubs" meet at Derby last week. He did two-four then.'

'Well, who else?'

'There's that Redbrooke, the Cambridge Blue. I ain't got an earthly.'

'He's a fine runner,' said Jones, 'but d'you think he's trained in May? Not likely; it'll be his first time out—trial spin like. Are you trained?'

'Pretty good,' said Andrew, 'been at it evenings all the month. Had a good race a week ago.'

'Take it from me,' Jones told him slowly, 'stick to Redbrooke. He'll come up at the end of the first quarter. You watch 'im. Don't mind what the others do. And don't run on the outside round bends.'

'Well, I know enough for that,' said Andrew.

'Ah, you know, you know,' said Jones. 'Well, good luck, lad.'

Andrew turned back again as he was going. 'If I could ever best two minutes,' he said, a little self-consciously, 'it'd mean—oh, well, a hellova lot.'

Andrew left him and went alone into the square garden to eat his sandwiches. It was a bright early summer day, yet now he was alone he felt chilly with nerves. He had a forty minutes' bus ride to the ground, and he meant to get there early. The half-mile was timed for three.

What chance had he got? He had won his heat in two-six the evening before, but that meant nothing. Joe Brewster was behind him, but he'd only paced it out, he knew. Perry and Redbrooke had tied the other heat in two-five. There was nothing to go by. Dreadful if he found himself outclassed and run off his legs. He had never been up against a class man before—a fellow like Redbrooke.

Once in the bus he tried his best not to think of the race.

No good getting too much of a needle. Yet it was a big chance.

Why, if he did well, if he was placed in the race today, his name would be in the *Sentinel*. The old 'uns would like to see that, too. If he could beat two minutes—well, he would some day, before he died. That would be doing something really big. It would give him confidence. It would make him stronger altogether.

The bus jogged along with such pleasant fancies. Andrew reached the ground, bag in hand, at half-past one. It gave him a queer feeling to see 'Sixpence Entrance' on the gates, and 'This stand a shilling', and the like. It made him feel very responsible that people should pay to come to the sport he was providing.

He was practically the firstcomer in the changing-room. He changed slowly, putting his clothes on a bench in the corner. He put on his spiked shoes with elaborate care and went out on to the track. It was three laps to the mile instead of the four he was used to. Pity: every strangeness was a little disturbing in a race. There were not four corners either, but two long straights with a long semi-circular sweep at each end.

Andrew found the half-mile start, and took his bearings. He trotted round half a lap, took one or two sprints, then some breathing exercises. He paced up the back-straight. That was where he must come up to the front. He determined to make a real sprinting start, and get an inside berth at all costs. No need for old Jones to tell him not to run on the outside round bends. It was past two by now. One or two people were coming into the stands, the first event being at 2.30. When he got back to the changing-room he found it full of a noisy jostling crowd. He felt rather strange and out of it. If only he could get it over. Three-quarters of an hour to wait still. On a table a naked body was being massaged. Andrew waited his turn for a rub. This seemed really professional.

'Your turn, sir,' said the rubber.

Andrew stripped off his vest.

'Might as well take your bags off, too.'

He divested himself a bit shyly, and lay face downwards on the table.

'Front side first, old man,' said the rubber.

It seemed a bit indecent, but Andrew turned over.

The man pummelled his stomach, then his back, then his buttocks, his thighs and his calves, rubbing in a strong smelling oil that gingered up his skin and made his nerves tingle. Good.

He saw Brewster and Perry talking and made a remark to them about the half-mile, but they did not seem to remember who he was. He found himself a seat alone. If only he could get it over.

A red-faced man thrust the door open.

'All out for the hundred,' he shouted.

'Know who that is?' someone said. 'That's Major Cunliffe—the old international.'

The hundred-yards men trooped out. There were four or five heats in the hundred. Andrew watched out of the changing-room window, but he couldn't concentrate and took no stock of what happened. He was acutely miserable.

At last the hundred yards was finished. A minute or so dragged by. Andrew stood up and sat down again and fastened his shoes for the fifth time. Then the door burst open and Major Cunliffe looked in again.

'All out for the half-mile!'

At the same time he heard a bell ringing outside. It sounded fateful. *It meant next event due.* All over the ground people were turning over their programmes and reading the names. As the clangour died away Andrew felt something approaching terror. He sprang to his feet and crossed towards the door.

Now a new awkwardness arose. Why did none of the other half-milers move? He waited for a moment for them to join him, but each man of them seemed to have found some last-minute adjustment to a shoe or bandage.

'Well,' said Brewster, 'I suppose we'd better be moving.'

'Wait a bit, Joe,' said Perry. 'I must get my ankle strap on.'

Andrew hovered miserably in the doorway of the changing-room. Why couldn't they buck up and get it over? If only he could get it over. At last, finding it ridiculous to hold the door open any longer, he went through it and waited outside in the concrete passage. He certainly could not walk on to the track without the others, nor could he go back into the changing-room. He leant against the wall trying to think of nothing.

What could the others be doing? 'Oh, come on,' he murmured, 'come on!' Next time he would know better than to get up before the other men in his race were on the move.

The sunlight end of the passage was suddenly eclipsed and the Major brushed by him.

'Where are those half-milers?' he said genially to Andrew.

'I think——' began Andrew, but found an answer was not expected.

The Major opened the door, and Andrew caught a glimpse of the bunch of them standing and talking as if the race meant nothing.

'Everyone out for the half-mile—come on, *please*,' said the Major.

This time they came, and with beating heart Andrew joined them.

'Well, Brewster,' said the Major, 'what are you going to show us today?'

'Don't expect you'll notice me,' said Brewster, 'after the gun's gone. I shall try and stick to young Redbrooke for the first six hundred, anyhow. I only want to see what I can do!'

It sounded splendidly casual, but Andrew had a strong feeling that what Brewster meant was: 'I rather fancy myself as a class half-miler, so just watch me. I believe I can beat Redbrooke. I'm not troubling about the rest, anyhow.'

Andrew stepped gingerly along the track. He felt rather better at being in the open air. Then he glanced behind him at the grandstand. He received a shock. It was full—full of banks of people looking at him, waiting to see him run.

With eyes fixed on the ground, he left the track and began to walk across the grass towards the start. The half-mile, being a lap and a half, led off at the farthest point from the grandstand. The half-lap brought it round to the

B

stand just at the stage where the race was getting into its
stride, when everybody was beginning to feel the collar
and those who meant business were jostling for places in
front. The remaining complete lap brought the finish
round to the grandstand again.

Andrew's path took him into the middle of the ground;
here the crowd was less imminent. The summer was still
new enough to greet the senses with surprise. He stepped
lightly on the elastic turf. The grass breathed out delicious
freshness. For years afterwards that fragrance was to set
Andrew's nerves tingling with the apprehension of this
moment.

The lively air fanned his head and throat. It played about
his bare legs.

Andrew saw the other half-milers were trotting round
the track. Occasionally one would shoot forward in a
muscle-stretching burst. Andrew tried a high-stepping trot
across the grass to flex his own legs, but was too self-
conscious to keep it up.

He reached the starting point first. Another agonizing
wait followed. The others were still capering round the
path. Would he never get it over? Surely the tension of
nerves must rack the strength from his limbs? At last the
starter approached.

'Jolly day for a trial spin,' he told Andrew. 'Makes me
feel an old fool to be out of it. I envy you boys.'

Andrew felt too miserable to answer. He nodded.

'If you want a place,' said the starter, 'take my advice and
watch Redbrooke. He'll probably try to take Brewster off
his legs early—he knows he can't sprint, you see.'

Andrew nodded again. Of course it was a foregone conclusion that only Redbrooke and Brewster were in the race. No one had a thought for him.

The others began to arrive. Andrew stripped off his sweater. Again he was premature. The others waited. All were silent now.

Redbrooke was strolling across the ground with one of the officials. He looked up and broke into a brisk trot. The air still freshened Andrew's face. Across the ground he could hear the murmur of the crowd. A paper-boy was shouting.

Still none of the runners spoke. In silence, one by one, they took off blazers and sweaters. The well-known colours of Brewster's club appeared—a red and black band round the chest. Redbrooke cantered up unconcerned.

'Sorry,' he said, and emerged from his blazer in Achilles Club colours. Andrew glanced at his plain white things, longer and tighter than Redbrooke's.

The runners eyed each other as they took their places on the track. Redbrooke was a shade taller than Andrew and perfectly formed. His corn-coloured hair was a dishevelled crop, paler in hue than the tan of his face. His limbs flashed with youth and strength. His poise was quick as flame.

No wonder he can run, thought Andrew. He must win.

'I shall say on your marks—set—and then fire.'

At last, thought Andrew. His heart was beating in his throat now.

A second toiled by.

Andrew dropped to his knee for a sprinting start. 'Set!'

His knee quivered up from the track. It was toes and knuckles now, a balance quivering with tautness.

CRASH.

Scurry. Shoulders jostling. Mind out.

Andrew shot clear, going at top speed. He swung into the inside place. So far, so good. He'd got his inside place, and the lead too. Was he to make the running? He settled down into a stride, fast but easy.

He breathed calmly through his nose. Although the race had started, he still felt very nervous—an exhilarating nervousness now. He saw each blade of grass where cut turf edge met track. A groundsman set down a whitewash pail.

Andrew realized he was cutting out too fast a pace. He swung into a slower stride. So far all had gone according to plan, and he began to take courage.

As they approached the pavilion for the first time and the second long corner of the race, he found Perry was creeping up on his outside. Andrew was surprised and a little worried. In all the half-miles he had run before the pace he had set would have assured him the lead. He decided to make no effort, and Perry passed stride by stride and dropped into the lead. Andrew continued at his own pace, and a gap of a yard or two opened.

As they came on to the bend there was a sudden sputter of feet and Andrew found that Brewster had filled the gap. Others were coming up, and he realized that the whole field was moving faster than he was. He quickened up slightly and swung out tentatively to pass Brewster again. Before he could pass the corner was reached. He at least knew better than to run on the outside round the curve; so he slackened again to pull back into the inside. But in the very thought of doing so, the runner behind closed smoothly and swiftly up to Brewster, and Andrew saw that Redbrooke had got his inside berth. Andrew had to take the curve on the outside. 'Blinking fool,' he told himself.

Old Jones and one or two other experienced runners in the crowd caught each other's eyes for a moment; the rest of the audience had no notion of the little display of bad technique that Andrew had given.

So they went round the long curve. Perry in the lead and still pressing the pace; Brewster second, with no very clear notion of what the pace ought to be, and determined not to lose Perry; Redbrooke keeping wisely within striking distance and Andrew bunched uncomfortably on the outside of Redbrooke with two others.

By the time they came out of the long bend and completed the first half of the race, Andrew was thoroughly rattled. Never had he felt such a strain at this stage of a half-mile. Already it was difficult to get enough air; he was no longer breathing evenly through his nose. Already a numbing weakness was creeping down the front of his thighs. Hopeless now to think of gaining ground. With relief he found he was able to drop into the inside again behind Redbrooke. They had been running now for about one minute—it seemed an age. Could he possibly stick to it for another period, as long again? The long stretch of straight in front of him, the long sweep of curve at the end of the ground that only brought you at the beginning of the finishing straight. Then the sprint. Already he felt he could not find an ounce of sprint.

Pace by pace he stuck to it, watching Redbrooke's feet.

But even now he must quicken up if he was to hold Redbrooke. At each step Redbrooke's back was leaving

Pace by pace he stuck to it, watching Redbrooke's feet

him. He struggled to lengthen, but it was useless. Red-brooke was moving up to the front. Now he was equal with Brewster; now with Perry; now he was in the lead. How easy Redbrooke's move down the back straight looked from the grandstand. 'Pretty running,' people told each other. 'Just the place to come up.' 'Nicely judged.' 'See how he worked himself through from the last corner.'

And this was the very place at which Andrew had meant to move up himself. He remembered nothing of his plans now. It was impossible to increase his effort. One of the men behind came smoothly by and dropped into the gap that Redbrooke had left in front of him. The sixth man came up on his outside. There was a kind of emptiness at his back. He was running equal last.

Now they came to the final curve before the finishing straight. His legs seemed powerless. He grunted for breath. The weakness in his thighs had grown to a cramp-ing pain. And all the time with full despair he saw Red-brooke going up, now five yards clear, now eight. Perry had dropped back to third, and Brewster was chasing Redbrooke.

Dark waves of pain swept over Andrew. Hopeless. Hopeless.

Still he must keep running with control. He must force his legs to a smooth long stride. This was the worst part of any race.

'Come on,' he told himself, 'another fifty yards—guts, man—guts.'

Had only Andrew known what the others were feeling, he would have taken courage. The whole pace of the first quarter, thanks to Andrew's own excitement had been faster than anyone cared for. Redbrooke, untrained as he was, had found himself badly winded at the quarter-mile mark. He, too, doubted whether he would have any punch left at the finish. He determined, therefore, to make a surprise effort early when he still had a powerful sprint in him. As soon as they came into the curve, he stepped on the gas as hard as he could, three hundred yards from home and steamed away. He jumped a lead of five, eight, ten yards before Perry or Brewster realized what was happening. It was a thing the crowd could follow better than the men in the race.

Now as they came into the straight, Andrew thought Redbrooke was gathering himself for a final dash. Far from it; he was hanging on for grim death. His sparkling effort had died right away. His stride was nerveless. The sprinting muscles in his thighs had lost every ounce of their power. He was struggling and asking himself at every stride: 'Can I, can I, can I—surely those steps are drawing nearer—can I last it?'

Perry was desperately run out. Brewster had already been chasing Redbrooke hard for the last thirty yards, but could not find any pace at all.

Andrew alone of the field had he known it had been nursing his remnant of strength round that gruelling bend. Only forty yards to go now and he could throw all he had into a last desperate effort. Keep it up just a moment more. Thirty yards to the straight now—twenty—suddenly his control was shattered. He was fighting in a mindless fury of effort for every ounce of strength in him.

In ten yards he saw his whole fortune in the race change. He *had* got a sprint, then! The man on his outside vanished.

He raced round the outside of the fellow in front hand over fist as he came into the straight. In another few yards he had the faltering Perry taped.

He had already run into third place. New strength urged through his limbs. 'Come on, come on: up, you can catch Brewster. Level. Feel him struggling. He can't hold you. Got him!'

Far, far off, a distant frenzied pain, somewhere; someone else's pain. Miles away a face on the side of the track.

Second now. Second, and he could catch Redbrooke. But could he catch him in time? They were past the start of the hundred yards now: a bare hundred to go. Could he? Could he? The first brilliance of his sprint had gone. He was fighting again in an agonizing weakness that dragged his legs back. But he was doing it, foot by foot. Fists clenched, to force speed-spent muscles.

Split seconds dragged strange length out. The straight went on and on. Five yards behind, now four, now three.

Redbrooke heard him, then felt him: two yards behind, now at his shoulder. He racked himself for a new effort. Together they swept past the hundred-yards finish, ten yards from the half-mile tape, with the dull roar of the crowd in their ears. Redbrooke saw he was beaten, but stuck to it till the last foot.

Then Andrew led.

A splendour of gladness as he watched the stretch of white wool break on his own chest.

'You've done it, you've done it!' Incredible, precious moment.

Then he dropped half-unconscious on the track.

Strong arms plucked him up and walked him to the grass.

'Well done, very fine finish,' he heard. Down again, sitting now. The world swam round you. There was Redbrooke, standing up—not so done, then.

Ache, how those legs ache, and your thigh muscles too—must stand up, hell, what does it matter though when you won!

Redbrooke came over to Andrew, smiling and controlled.

'Well done,' he said, 'you had me nicely.'

'Ow,' said Andrew, still panting, 'muscles in my thighs.' He got up and limped about. His legs felt absurd. The muscles in his haunches hurt abominably.

Redbrooke smiled. 'I know that feeling,' he said, 'comes of running untrained.'

'Oh, I had trained a bit,' said Andrew, 'a fair amount really. Do you know what the time was?'

'One fifty-nine and two-fifths,' Redbrooke told him. 'I was just inside two minutes. I must say I think we did fairly well for the first effort of the season.'

'One fifty-nine and two-fifths,' said Andrew, 'was it really?'

One of the judges joined them.

Others came up. They all said the same.

'Why on earth didn't you sprint before?'

'No idea I could,' explained Andrew.

Brewster joined the group.

'Well, that's my last half-mile,' he said. 'Never had to move so fast in my life before.'

But he was obviously pleased. He had finished about ten

yards behind Redbrooke and must have done about two-two or two-three.

Now Andrew began to enjoy himself thoroughly. Gloriously relaxed in mind and body, gloriously contented, he watched the other events. He made new friends. Then he went in and soaked himself in a steaming bath and smoked, shouting to Brewster in the next compartment. Life was very kind.

He came out on to the ground, chatted with everyone he saw; discussed his race a dozen times: had three or four beers: spent a few shillings with extravagance. He saw, to his amazement, Redbrooke turn out again for the quarter and fight another gruelling finish to win by inches in fifty-one and a fifth seconds. Andrew was the first to pat him on the back.

'Great work,' he said. 'How you managed it after that half beats me!'

'Oh, well,' said Redbrooke, 'it loosened me up. Why didn't you come, lazy devil?'

In the bus going home, Andrew leant back and puffed deeply at his pipe. Alone for the first time, he went over the race in his mind. Well, he had done it. He could tackle anything on earth now.

After all, running was a thing men had always done. Football, other games, came and went. A good runner was a good runner for all time—with hundreds and hundreds of years of kinship behind him. And he, Andrew, was a good runner. A class runner. One fifty-nine. Damn good!

His head was slightly swimming with fatigue and excitement and beer. He leant back and sighed—as happy as it is possible to be on this planet.

A MILD ATTACK OF LOCUSTS

*Since the days of the eighth plague of Egypt, when locusts
'covered the whole earth, so that the land was darkened', men
have recorded with horror the devastations caused by their swarms.*

*What are locusts, and why are they such a plague to man?
Locusts are short-horn grasshoppers, differing from the familiar
and less destructive grasshoppers of English summer hedgerows in
that they are larger and love to wander great distances in crowds.
The locust larvae, or hoppers, collect together in tens of thousands
and wander about the countryside in armies, moving sometimes a
mile in twenty-four hours. Fully grown locusts collect in swarms
and fly several miles a day. When they settle, they eat every
living plant about them, an average-sized swarm devouring
about twenty tons of food a day.*

*Today governments are fighting this age-long scourge with
modern methods of pest control. Areas where outbreaks of locusts
occur are sprayed with insecticides such as Gammexane and
Dieldrin. Farmers are warned by radio of the approach of
swarms. Yet when the swarms are blackening the sky overhead,
farmers still resort to the primitive and ineffective device of
banging gongs and lighting fires to discourage the locusts from
settling.**

The scene of this story is set in central Africa.

THE RAINS that year were good, they were coming nicely
just as the crops needed them—or so Margaret gathered

* (Adapted from *The Oxford Junior Encyclopaedia*.)

28

when the men said they were not too bad. She never had an opinion of her own on matters like the weather, because even to know about what seems a simple thing like the weather needs experience. Which Margaret had not got. The men were Richard her husband, and old Stephen, Richard's father, a farmer from way back, and these two might argue for hours whether the rains were ruinous, or just ordinarily exasperating. Margaret had been on the farm three years. She still did not understand how they did not go bankrupt altogether, when the men never had a good word for the weather, or the soil, or the Government. But she was getting to learn the language. Farmer's language. And they neither went bankrupt nor got very rich. They jogged along, doing comfortably.

Their crop was maize. Their farm was three thousand acres on the ridges that rise up towards the Zambezi escarpment, high, dry windswept country, cold and dusty in winter, but now, being the wet season, steamy with the heat rising in wet, soft waves off miles of green foliage. Beautiful it was, with the sky blue and brilliant halls of air, and the bright green folds and hollows of country beneath, and the mountains lying sharp and bare twenty miles off across the rivers. The sky made her eyes ache, she was not used to it. One does not look so much at the sky in the city she came from. So that evening when Richard said: 'The Government is sending out warnings that locusts are expected, coming down from the breeding grounds up North,' her instinct was to look about her at the trees. Insects—swarms of them—horrible! But Richard and the old man had raised their eyes and were looking up over the mountains. 'We haven't had locusts in seven years,' they said. 'They go in cycles, locusts do.' And then: 'There goes our crop for this season!'

But they went on with the work of the farm just as usual, until one day they were coming up the road to the homestead for the midday break, when old Stephen stopped, raised his finger and pointed: 'Look, look, there they are!'

Out ran Margaret to join them, looking at the hills. Out came the servants from the kitchen. They all stood and gazed. Over the rocky levels of the mountain was a streak of rust-coloured air. Locusts. There they came.

At once Richard shouted at the cook-boy. Old Stephen yelled at the house-boy. The cook-boy ran to beat the old ploughshare hanging from a tree-branch, which was used to summon the labourers at moments of crisis. The house-boy ran off to the store to collect tin cans, any old bit of metal. The farm was ringing with the clamour of the gong, and they could see the labourers come pouring out of the compound, pointing at the hills and shouting excitedly. Soon they had all come up to the house, and Richard and old Stephen were giving them orders—Hurry, hurry, hurry.

And off they ran again, the two white men with them, and in a few minutes Margaret could see the smoke of fires rising from all around the farm-lands. Piles of wood and grass had been prepared there. There were seven patches of bared soil, yellow and ox-blood colour, and pink, where the new mealies were just showing, making a film of bright green, and around each drifted up thick clouds of smoke. They were throwing wet leaves on to the fires now, to make it acrid and black. Margaret was watching the hills. Now there was a long, low cloud advancing, rust-colour still, swelling forward and out as she looked. The telephone was ringing. Neighbours—quick, quick, there come the locusts. Old Smith had had his crop eaten to the ground. Quick, get your fires started. For of course, while every farmer hoped the locusts would overlook his farm and go on to the next, it was only fair to warn each other, one must play fair. Everywhere, fifty miles over the countryside, the smoke was rising from myriads of fires. Margaret answered the telephone calls, and between stood watching the locusts. The air was darkening. A strange darkness, for the sun was blazing—it was like the darkness of a veldt fire, when the air gets thick with smoke. The sunlight comes down distorted, a thick hot orange. Oppressive it was, too, with the heaviness of a storm. The locusts were coming fast. Now half the sky was darkened. Behind the reddish veils in front which were the advance guards of the swarm, the main swarm showed in dense black cloud, reaching almost to the sun itself.

Margaret was wondering what she could do to help. She did not know. Then up came old Stephen from the lands. 'We're finished, Margaret, finished! Those beggars can eat every leaf and blade off the farm in half an hour! And it is only early afternoon—if we can make enough smoke, make enough noise till the sun goes down, they'll settle somewhere else perhaps. . . .' And then: 'Get the kettle going. It's thirsty work, this.'

So Margaret went to the kitchen, and stoked up the fire, and boiled the water. Now, on the tin roof of the kitchen she could hear the thuds and bangs of falling locusts, or a scratching slither as one skidded down. Here were the first of them. From down on the lands came the beating and banging and clanging of a hundred petrol tins and bits of metal. Stephen impatiently waited while one petrol tin was filled with tea, hot, sweet and orange-coloured, and the other with water. In the meantime, he told Margaret about how twenty years back he was eaten out, made bankrupt by the locust armies. And then, still talking, he hoisted up the petrol cans, one in each hand, by the wood pieces set corner-wise across each, and jogged off down to the road to the thirsty labourers. By now the locusts were falling like hail on to the roof of the kitchen. It sounded like a heavy storm. Margaret looked out and saw the air dark with a criss-cross of the insects, and she set her teeth and ran out into it—what the men could do, she could. Overhead the air was thick, locusts everywhere. The locusts were flopping against her and she brushed them off, heavy red-brown creatures, looking at her with their beady old-men's eyes while they clung with hard serrated legs. She held her breath with disgust and ran through into the house. There it was even more like being in a heavy storm. The iron roof was reverberating, and the clamour of iron from the lands was like thunder. Looking out, all the trees were queer and still, clotted with insects, their boughs weighed to the ground. The earth seemed to be moving, locusts crawling everywhere, she could not see the lands at all, so thick was the swarm. Towards the mountains it was like looking into driving rain—even as she watched, the sun was blotted out with a fresh onrush of them. It was a half-night, a perverted blackness. Then came a sharp crack from the bush—a branch had snapped off. Then another. A tree down the slope leaned over and settled heavily to the ground. Through the hail of insects a man came running. More tea, more water was needed. She supplied them. She kept the fires stoked and filled tins with liquid, and then it was four in the afternoon, and the locusts had been pouring across overhead for a couple of hours. Up came old Stephen again, crunching locusts underfoot with every step, locusts clinging all over him, cursing and swearing, banging with his old hat in the air. At the doorway he stopped briefly, hastily pulling at the clinging insects and throwing them off, then he plunged into the locust-free living-room.

'All the crops finished. Nothing left,' he said.

But the gongs were still beating, the men still shouting, and Margaret asked: 'Why do you go on with it, then?'

'The main swarm isn't settling. They are heavy with eggs. They are looking for a place to settle and lay. If we can stop the main body settling on our farm, that's every-thing. If they get a chance to lay their eggs, we are going to have everything eaten flat with hoppers later on.' He picked a stray locust off his shirt, and split it down with his thumb-nail—it was clotted inside with eggs. 'Imagine that multiplied by millions. You ever seen a hopper swarm on the march? Well, you're lucky.'

Margaret thought that an adult swarm was bad enough. Outside now the light on the earth was a pale thin yellow, clotted with moving shadow, the clouds of moving insects thickened and lightened like driving rain. Old Stephen said: 'They've got the wind behind them, that's some-thing.'

'Is it very bad?' asked Margaret fearfully, and the old man said emphatically: 'We're finished. This swarm may pass over, but once they've started, they'll be coming

c

down from the North now one after another. And then there are the hoppers—it might go on for two or three years.'

Margaret sat down helplessly, and thought: 'Well, if it's the end, it's the end. What now? We'll all three have to go back to town . . .' But at this, she took a quick look at Stephen, the old man who had farmed forty years in this country, been bankrupt twice, and she knew nothing would make him go and become a clerk in the city. Yet her heart ached for him, he looked so tired, the worry-lines deep from nose to mouth. Poor old man. . . . He had lifted up a locust that had got itself somehow into his pocket, holding it in the air by one leg. 'You've got the strength of a steel-spring in those legs of yours,' he was telling the locust, good-humouredly. Then although he had been fighting locusts, squashing locusts, yelling at locusts, sweeping them in great mounds into the fires to burn for the last three hours, nevertheless he took this one to the door, and carefully threw it out to join its fellows as if he would rather not harm a hair of its head. This comforted Margaret, all at once she felt irrationally cheered. She remembered it was not the first time in the last three years the men had announced their final and irremediable ruin.

'Get me a drink, lass,' he then said, and she set the bottle of whisky by him.

In the meantime, out in the pelting storm of insects, her husband was banging the gong, feeding the fires with leaves, the insects clinging to him all over—she shuddered. 'How can you bear to let them touch you?' she asked. He looked at her, disapproving. She felt suitably humble—

just as she had when he had first taken a good look at her city self, hair waved and golden, nails red and pointed. Now she was a proper farmer's wife, in sensible shoes and a solid skirt. She might even get to letting locusts settle on her—in time.

Having tossed back a whisky or two, old Stephen went back into the battle, wading now through glistening brown waves of locusts.

Five o'clock. The sun would set in an hour. Then the swarm would settle. It was as thick overhead as ever. The trees were ragged mounds of glistening brown.

Margaret began to cry. It was all so hopeless—if it wasn't a bad season, it was locusts, if it wasn't locusts, it was army-worm, or veldt fires. Always something. The rustling of the locust armies was like a big forest in the storm, their settling on the roof was like the beating of the rain, the ground was invisible in a sleek brown surging tide—it was like being drowned in locusts, submerged by the loathsome brown flood. It seemed as if the roof might sink in under the weight of them, as if the door might give in under their pressure and these rooms fill with them—and it was getting so dark . . . she looked up. The air was thinner, gaps of blue showed in the dark moving clouds. The blue spaces were cold and thin: the sun must be setting. Through the fog of insects she saw figures approaching. First old Stephen, marching bravely along, then her husband, drawn and haggard with weariness. Behind them the servants. All were crawling all over with insects. The sound of the gongs had stopped. She could hear nothing but the ceaseless rustle of a myriad wings.

The two men slapped off the insects and came in.

'Well,' said Richard, kissing her on the cheek, 'the main swarm has gone over.'

'For the Lord's sake,' said Margaret angrily, still half-crying, 'what's here is bad enough, isn't it?' For although the evening air was no longer black and thick, but a clear blue, with a pattern of insects whizzing this way and that across it, everything else—trees, buildings, bushes, earth, was gone under the moving brown masses.

'If it doesn't rain in the night and keep them here—if it doesn't rain and weigh them down with water, they'll be off in the morning at sunrise.'

'We're bound to have some hoppers. But not the main swarm, that's something.'

Margaret roused herself, wiped her eyes, pretended she had not been crying, and fetched them some supper, for the servants were too exhausted to move. She sent them down to the compound to rest.

She served the supper and sat listening. There is not one maize-plant left, she heard. Not one. The men would get the planters out the moment the locusts had gone. They must start all over again.

'But what's the use of that?' Margaret wondered, if the whole farm was going to be crawling with hoppers? But she listened while they discussed the new Government pamphlet which said how to defeat the hoppers. You must have men out all the time moving over the farm to watch for movement in the grass. When you find a patch of hoppers, small lively black things, like crickets, then you dig trenches around the patch, or spray them with poison from pumps supplied by the Government. The Government wanted them to co-operate in a world plan for eliminating this plague for ever. You should attack locusts at the source. Hoppers, in short. The men were talking as if they were planning a war, and Margaret listened, amazed.

In the night it was quiet, no sign of the settled armies outside, except sometimes a branch snapped, or a tree could be heard crashing down.

Margaret slept badly in the bed beside Richard, who was sleeping like the dead, exhausted with the afternoon's fight. In the morning she woke to yellow sunshine lying across the bed, clear sunshine, with an occasional blotch of shadow moving over it. She went to the window. Old Stephen was ahead of her. Then he stood outside, gazing down over the bush. And she gazed, astounded—and entranced, much against her will. For it looked as if every tree, every bush, all the earth, were lit with pale flames. The locusts were fanning their wings to free them of the night dews. There was a shimmer of red-tinged gold light everywhere.

She went out to join the old man, stepping carefully among the insects. They stood and watched. Overhead the sky was blue, blue and clear.

'Pretty,' said old Stephen with satisfaction.

Well, thought Margaret, we may be ruined, we may be bankrupt, but not everyone has seen an army of locusts fanning their wings at dawn.

Over the slopes, in the distance, a faint red smear showed in the sky, thickened and spread. 'There they go,' said old Stephen. 'There goes the main army, off South.'

And now from the trees, from the earth all round them, the locusts were taking wing. They were like small aircraft, manoeuvring for the take-off, trying their wings to see if they were dry enough. Off they went. A reddish brown steam was rising off the miles of bush, off the lands, the earth. Again the sunlight darkened.

And as the clotted branches lifted, the weight on them lightening, there was nothing but the black spines of branches, trees. No green left, nothing. All morning they watched, the three of them, as the brown crust thinned and broke and dissolved, flying up to mass with the main army, now a brownish-red smear in the Southern sky. The lands which had been filmed with green, the new tender mealie plants, were stark and bare. All the trees stripped. A devastated landscape. No green, no green anywhere.

By midday the reddish cloud had gone. Only an occasional locust flopped down. On the ground were the corpses and the wounded. The African labourers were sweeping these up with branches and collecting them in tins.

'Ever eaten sun-dried locust?' asked old Stephen. 'That time twenty years ago, when I went broke, I lived on mealiemeal and dried locusts for three months. They aren't bad at all—rather like smoked fish, if you come to think of it.'

But Margaret preferred not even to think of it.

After the midday meal the men went off to the lands. Everything was to be replanted. With a bit of luck another swarm would not come travelling down just this way. But they hoped it would rain very soon, to spring some new grass, because the cattle would die otherwise—there was not a blade of grass left on the farm. As for Margaret, she was trying to get used to the idea of three or four years of locusts. Locusts were going to be like bad weather, from now on, always imminent. She felt like a survivor after war—if this devastated and mangled countryside was not ruin, well, what then was ruin?

But the men ate their supper with good appetites.

'It could have been worse,' was what they said. 'It could be much worse.'

THE FOG HORN

Over a hundred million years ago the Earth was peopled with primitive animals of fantastic shape. Plesiosaurs with barrel-shaped bodies thirty foot long paddled heavily through the seas with their four flat legs. Overhead glided pterodactyls casting weird shadows on the hills as their twenty foot wings came between the Sun and the Earth. On land the huge Megalosaurus ran about on his clawed hind legs, raising his head into the middle branches of the giant fern trees.

Geologists have known for many years that such monsters existed, because they have found the imprint of their bones preserved in ancient rocks. What is surprising to scientists, however, is the recent discovery that some prehistoric creatures, which had long been considered extinct, are still to be found in the depths of the oceans. In 1938 some fishermen off the coast of South Africa caught a coelacanth, a primitive fish thought to have become extinct sixty million years ago. In 1952 a Danish zoological expedition to the Pacific discovered an archaic mollusc two miles under the sea, a mollusc which is known to have existed over three hundred million years ago.

What if, in the unplumbed deeps of ocean, an even larger pre-historic beast still dwells—some monstrous marine dinosaur—yet to be awakened from his 'ancient, dreamless, uninvaded sleep', a creature who will one night raise his mighty head and neck out of our own familiar coastal waters and strike primeval terror into the hearts of men?

OUT THERE in the cold water, far from land, we waited every night for the coming of the fog, and it came, and we oiled the brass machinery and lit the fog light up in the stone tower. Feeling like two birds in the grey sky, McDunn and I sent the light touching out, red, then white, then red again, to eye the lonely ships. And if they did not see our light, then there was always our Voice, the great deep cry of our Fog Horn shuddering through the rags of mist to startle the gulls away like packs of scattered cards and make the waves turn high and foam.

'It's a lonely life, but you're used to it now, aren't you?' asked McDunn.

'Yes,' I said. 'You're a good talker, thank the Lord.'

'Well, it's your turn on land tomorrow,' he said, smiling, 'to dance the ladies and drink gin.'

'What do you think, McDunn, when I leave you out here alone?'

'On the mysteries of the sea.' McDunn lit his pipe. It was a quarter past seven of a cold November evening, the heat on, the light switching its tail in two hundred directions, the Fog Horn bumbling in the high throat of the tower. There wasn't a town for a hundred miles down the coast, just a road which came lonely through dead country to the sea, with few cars on it, a stretch of two miles of cold water out to our rock, and rare few ships.

'The mysteries of the sea,' said McDunn thoughtfully. 'You know, the ocean's the biggest damned snowflake ever? It rolls and swells a thousand shapes and colours, no two alike. Strange. One night, years ago, I was here alone, when all of the fish of the sea surfaced out there.

Something made them swim in and lie in the bay, sort of trembling and staring up at the tower light going red, white, red, white across them so I could see their funny eyes. I turned cold. They were like a big peacock's tail, moving out there until midnight. Then, without so much as a sound, they slipped away, the million of them was gone. I kind of think maybe, in some sort of way, they came all those miles to worship. Strange. But think how the tower must look to them, standing seventy feet above the water, the God-light flashing out from it, and the tower declaring itself with a monster voice. They never came back, those fish, but don't you think for a while they thought they were in the Presence?'

I shivered. I looked out at the long grey lawn of the sea stretching away into nothing and nowhere.

'Oh, the sea's full.' McDunn puffed his pipe nervously, blinking. He had been nervous all day and hadn't said why. 'For all our engines and so-called submarines, it'll be ten thousand centuries before we set foot on the real bottom of the sunken lands, in the fairy kingdoms there, and know *real* terror. Think of it, it's still the year 300,000 Before Christ down under there. While we've paraded around with trumpets, lopping off each other's countries and heads, they have been living beneath the sea twelve miles deep and cold in a time as old as the beard of a comet.'

'Yes, it's an old world.'

'Come on. I got something special I been saving up to tell you.'

We ascended the eighty steps, talking and taking our time. At the top, McDunn switched off the room lights so there'd be no reflection in the plate glass. The great eye of the light was humming, turning easily in its oiled socket. The Fog Horn was blowing steadily, once every fifteen seconds.

'Sounds like an animal, don't it?' McDunn nodded to himself. 'A big lonely animal crying in the night. Sitting here on the edge of ten billion years calling out to the Deeps, I'm here, I'm here, I'm here. And the Deeps *do* answer, yes, they do. You been here now for three months, Johnny, so I better prepare you. About this time of year,' he said, studying the murk and fog, 'something comes to visit the lighthouse.'

'The swarms of fish like you said?'

'No, this is something else. I've put off telling you because you might think I'm daft. But tonight's the latest I can put it off, for if my calendar's marked right from last year, tonight's the night it comes. I won't go into detail, you'll have to see it yourself. Just sit down there. If you want, tomorrow you can pack your duffel and take the motorboat in to land and get your car parked there at the dinghy pier on the cape and drive on back to some little inland town and keep your lights burning nights, I won't question or blame you. It's happened three years now, and this is the only time anyone's been here with me to verify it. You wait and watch.'

Half an hour passed with only a few whispers between us. When we grew tired waiting, McDunn began describing some of his ideas to me. He had some theories about the Fog Horn itself.

'One day many years ago a man walked along and stood in the sound of the ocean on a cold sunless shore and said, "We need a voice to call across the water, to warn ships;

I'll make one. I'll make a voice like all of time and all of the
fog that ever was; I'll make a voice that is like an empty
bed beside you all night long, and like an empty house
when you open the door, and like trees in autumn with no
leaves. A sound like the birds flying south, crying, and a
sound like November wind and the sea on the hard, cold
shore. I'll make a sound that's so alone that no one can miss
it, that whoever hears it will weep in their souls, and hearths
will seem warmer, and being inside will seem better to all
who hear it in the distant towns. I'll make me a sound and
an apparatus and they'll call it a Fog Horn and whoever
hears it will know the sadness of eternity and the briefness
of life."'

The Fog Horn blew.

'I made up that story,' said McDunn quietly, 'to try to
explain why this thing keeps coming back to the lighthouse
every year. The Fog Horn calls it, I think, and it comes . . .'

'But——' I said.

'Sssst!' said McDunn. 'There!' He nodded out to the
Deeps.

Something was swimming towards the lighthouse
tower.

It was a cold night, as I have said; the high tower was
cold, the light coming and going, and the Fog Horn calling
and calling through the ravelling mist. You couldn't see
far and you couldn't see plain, but there was the deep sea
moving on its way about the night earth, flat and quiet, the
colour of grey mud, and here were the two of us alone in
the high tower, and there, far out at first, was a ripple, followed by a wave, a rising, a bubble, a bit of froth. And
then, from the surface of the cold sea came a head, a large

head, dark-coloured, with immense eyes, and then a neck. And then—not a body—but more neck and more! The head rose a full forty feet above the water on a slender and beautiful dark neck. Only then did the body, like a little island of black coral and shells and cray-fish, drip up from the subterranean. There was a flicker of tail. In all, from head to tip of tail, I estimated the monster at ninety or a hundred feet.

I don't know what I said. I said something.

'Steady, boy, steady,' whispered McDunn.

'It's impossible!' I said.

'No, Johnny, *we're* impossible. *It's* like it always was ten million years ago. *It* hasn't changed. It's *us* and the land that've changed, become impossible. *Us!*'

It swam slowly and with a great dark majesty out in the icy waters, far away. The fog came and went about it, momentarily erasing its shape. One of the monster eyes caught and held and flashed back our immense light, red, white, red, white, like a disc held high and sending a message in primeval code. It was as silent as the fog through which it swam.

'It's a dinosaur of some sort!' I crouched down, holding to the stair rail.

'Yes, one of the tribe.'

'But they died out!'

'No, only hid away in the Deeps. Deep, deep down in the deepest Deeps. Isn't *that* a word now, Johnny, a real word, it says so much: the Deeps. There's all the coldness and darkness and deepness in the world in a word like that.'

'What'll we do?'

'Do? We got our job, we can't leave. Besides, we're

safer here than in any boat trying to get to land. That thing's as big as a destroyer and almost as swift.'

'But here, why does it come *here*?'

The next moment I had my answer.

The Fog Horn blew.

And the monster answered.

A cry came across a million years of water and mist. A cry so anguished and alone that it shuddered in my head and my body. The monster cried out at the tower. The Fog Horn blew. The monster roared again. The Fog Horn blew. The monster opened its great toothed mouth and the sound that came from it was the sound of the Fog Horn itself. Lonely and vast and far away. The sound of isolation, a viewless sea, a cold night, apartness. That was the sound.

'Now!' whispered McDunn, 'do you know why it comes here?'

I nodded.

'All year long, Johnny, that poor monster there lying far out, a thousand miles at sea, and twenty miles deep maybe, biding its time, perhaps it's a million years old, this one creature. Think of it, waiting a million years; could *you* wait that long? Maybe it's the last of its kind. I sort of think that's true. Anyway, here come men on land and build this lighthouse, five years ago. And set up their Fog Horn and sound it out towards the place where you bury yourself in sleep and sea memories of a world where there were thousands like yourself, but now you're alone, all alone in a world not made for you, a world where you have to hide.

'But the sound of the Fog Horn comes and goes, comes and goes, and you stir from the muddy bottom of the

Deeps, and your eyes open like the lenses of two-foot cameras and you move, slow, slow, for you have the ocean sea on your shoulders, heavy. But that Fog Horn comes through a thousand miles of water, faint and familiar, and the furnace in your belly stokes up, and you begin to rise, slow, slow. You feed yourself on great slakes of cod and minnow, on rivers of jellyfish, and you rise slow through the autumn months, through September when the fogs started, through October with more fog and the horn still calling you on, and then, late in November, after pressurizing yourself day by day, a few feet higher every hour, you are near the surface and still alive. You've got to go slow; if you surfaced all at once you'd explode. So it takes you all of three months to surface, and then a number of days to swim through the cold waters to the lighthouse. And there you are, out there, in the night, Johnny, the biggest damn monster in creation. And here's the lighthouse calling to you, with a long neck like your neck sticking way up out of the water, and a body like your body, and, most important of all, a voice like your voice. Do you understand now, Johnny, do you understand?'

The Fog Horn blew.

The monster answered.

I saw it all, I knew it all—the million years of waiting alone, for someone to come back who never came back. The million years of isolation at the bottom of the sea, the insanity of time there, while the skies cleared of reptile-birds, the swamps dried on the continental lands, the sloths and sabre-tooths had their day and sank in tar pits, and men ran like white ants upon the hills.

The Fog Horn blew.

'Last year,' said McDunn, 'that creature swam round and round, round and round, all night. Not coming too near, puzzled, I'd say. Afraid, maybe. And a bit angry after coming all this way. But the next day, unexpectedly, the fog lifted, the sun came out fresh, the sky was blue as a painting. And the monster swam off away from the heat and the silence and didn't come back. I suppose it's been brooding on it for a year now, thinking it over from every which way.'

The monster was only a hundred yards off now, it and the Fog Horn crying at each other. As the lights hit them, the monster's eyes were fire and ice, fire and ice.

'That's life for you,' said McDunn. 'Someone always waiting for someone who never comes home. Always someone loving something more than that thing loves them. And after a while you want to destroy whatever that thing is, so it can't hurt you no more.'

The monster was rushing at the lighthouse.

The Fog Horn blew.

'Let's see what happens,' said McDunn.

He switched the Fog Horn off.

The ensuing minute of silence was so intense that we could hear our hearts pounding in the glassed area of the tower, could hear the slow greased turn of the light.

The monster stopped and froze. It's great lantern eyes blinked. Its mouth gaped. It gave a sort of rumble, like a volcano. It twitched its head this way and that, as if to seek the sounds now dwindled off into the fog. It peered at the lighthouse. It rumbled again. Then its eyes caught fire. It reared up, threshed the water, and rushed at the tower, its eyes filled with angry torment.

It reared up, threshed the water, and rushed at the tower

D

'McDunn!' I cried. 'Switch on the horn!'

McDunn fumbled with the switch. But even as he flicked it on the monster was rearing up. I had a glimpse of its gigantic paws, fishskin glittering in webs between the fingerlike projections, clawing at the tower. The huge eye on the right side of its anguished head glittered before me like a cauldron into which I might drop, screaming. The tower shook. The Fog Horn cried; the monster cried. It seized the tower and gnashed at the glass, which shattered in upon us.

McDunn seized my arm. 'Downstairs!'

The tower rocked, trembled, and started to give. The Fog Horn and the monster roared. We stumbled and half fell down the stairs. 'Quick!'

We reached the bottom as the tower buckled down towards us. We ducked under the stairs into the small stone cellar. There were a thousand concussions as the rocks rained down; the Fog Horn stopped abruptly. The monster crashed upon the tower. The tower fell. We knelt together, McDunn and I, holding tight, while our world exploded.

Then it was over, and there was nothing but darkness and the wash of the sea on the raw stones.

That and the other sound.

'Listen,' said McDunn quietly. 'Listen.'

We waited a moment. And then I began to hear it. First a great vacuumed sucking of air, and then the lament, the bewilderment, the loneliness of the great monster, folded over and upon us, above us, so that the sickening reek of its body filled the air, a stone's thickness away from our cellar. The monster gasped and cried. The tower was gone. The light was gone. The thing that had called to it across a million years was gone. And the monster was opening its mouth and sending out great sounds. The sounds of a Fog Horn, again and again. And ships far at sea, not finding the light, not seeing anything, but passing and hearing late that night, must've thought: There it is, the lonely sound, the Lonesome Bay horn. All's well. We've rounded the cape.

And so it went for the rest of that night.

The sun was hot and yellow the next afternoon when the rescuers came out to dig us from our stoned-under cellar.

'It fell apart, is all,' said Mr McDunn gravely. 'We had a few bad knocks from the waves and it just crumbled.' He pinched my arm.

There was nothing to see. The ocean was calm, the sky blue. The only thing was a great algaic stink from the green matter that covered the fallen tower stones and the shore rocks. Flies buzzed about. The ocean washed empty on the shore.

The next year they built a new lighthouse, but by that time I had a job in the little town and a wife and a good small warm house that glowed yellow on autumn nights, the doors locked, the chimney puffing smoke. As for McDunn, he was master of the new lighthouse, built to his own specifications, out of steel-reinforced concrete. 'Just in case,' he said.

The new lighthouse was ready in November. I drove down alone one evening late and parked my car and looked across the grey waters and listened to the new horn sounding, once, twice, three, four times a minute far out there, by itself.

The monster?

It never came back.

'It's gone away,' said McDunn. 'It's gone back to the Deeps. It's learned you can't love anything too much in this world. It's gone into the deepest Deeps to wait another million years. Ah, the poor thing! Waiting out here, and waiting out there, while man comes and goes on this pitiful little planet. Waiting and waiting.'

I sat in my car, listening. I couldn't see the lighthouse or the light standing out in Lonesome Bay. I could only hear the Horn, the Horn, the Horn. It sounded like the monster calling.

I sat there wishing there was something I could say.

THE HOSTAGES

This story is about three Etruscan boys who lived in Italy during the fourth century B.C. At the height of their power in 500 B.C. the Etruscans had ruled about a third of the Italian peninsula, but with the rise of Rome the Etruscans had lost one city after another to the new power. At the time of this story the Etruscan League of Cities had broken a treaty with the Romans. In the fighting that follows, a Roman legion, having taken many Etruscans hostage, finds itself besieged in a walled town. To break the courage of the Etruscan besiegers, the Romans flog their hostages on the town walls within sight of their kinsmen.

THERE WERE only three of us left now; the others had been hung over the ramparts, one every morning. Elxsente was still sick and we didn't know what to do with him; he was only a child, and cried for his mother at nights; some of the others had done that, and I would have too, but I was fifteen and had to set a good example. They used to take us out on to the walls, and whip us where the men from our own Cities could see us; of course they had the right to do it, but some of us weren't very old, and used to cry even at the thought of it, which was bad for everyone. But we could look out when we were taken up, and there was our camp, spread and shining below us; once there was an attack while we were there and we all cheered, but the Romans paid us back in kicks for that. I saw the banner of Mireto from time to time, and thought I could make out my father at the head of the spearmen, and my big brother with him; and once I saw a herald whom I knew, and called out to him, but he didn't hear me. Every day we hoped the town would fall, though we should very likely have been killed before any one could get to us; still, it was a chance, and better than being dragged out and choked like dogs at the end of a rope. We knew our people were pressing hard and might soon starve the town out; for the last week they had given us nothing but water and very little bread; the one who was chosen to be hung every morning used to leave his share of the bread to any one he liked. There wasn't too much water, either; the last day Teffre and I had given it all to Elxsente; we thought we should be able to eat his bread—he wouldn't touch it—but we were too thirsty.

I was awake all that night, though Teffre slept for a little. I leant up against the wall at the back, with Elxsente's head on my shoulder; he seemed easier that way. I thought about home, and tried to imagine I was in my own room; I wondered if they were looking after my pony properly, and I tried to remember whether I'd mended the bridle before I was sent away as a hostage to the Romans; I couldn't be sure, and it worried me.

When it was just light Teffre woke up and said he heard shouting; we both listened and I heard it too. He went over to the slit, but of course he could see nothing; he used always to think he might see something some time. But certainly there was cheering and Teffre said he was sure we'd taken the town; but it wasn't the first time he'd thought that and I wasn't hopeful, particularly as nothing else happened for hours. My back was very sore from the beating, and we'd had no chance of a wash for weeks. Elxsente was better after his sleep, and thirsty, but the water was all gone.

Then the door opened, and the man we called the Boar —we all hated him—came in. I wondered which of us he was going to take, and rather hoped it would be Teffre, because I was much better at looking after Elxsente—I didn't want it to be *him* anyhow. Teffre asked him what had happened—he never could learn not to—and the man hit his hand with the iron key, and then said, 'The General's come, and your people have all run away.' That was hard hearing for us; we knew it wasn't true about our army having run, but we supposed they'd withdrawn, and we were very unhappy, but we said nothing and waited. He went on: 'You dogs, you ought to be hung, but the General's begged your lives and you've been given to him.'

We didn't quite understand at once, and then a great tall man came in, all in armour, with a golden helmet plumed with a black horse-tail; he could only stand upright in the middle of the arch; he looked at us and asked, 'Are these all that are left?' The Boar stood at attention as he said, 'Yes, sir,' and then to us: 'Down on your knees before your master!' I don't remember what Teffre did, but I simply sat and stared at the General; one can't think very quickly after one hasn't slept all night. The Boar came over and hit me and I was afraid he was going to hit Elxsente; so I knelt, and Elxsente knelt, leaning against me, and Teffre knelt in the other corner. The light came in through the doorway, behind the General, and he looked very big, as if he could tread us into the ground; a little wind came in too and I heard the horse-hairs rustling against the bronze.

He was speaking to us, but I didn't hear it all; I was thinking that we were going to live, and I was glad and thankful, and then I thought that our army was beaten, and perhaps my father and brother were killed; I felt that I loved Mireto, my city, terribly, and that it would be awful if the Romans were to take her; and then I thought it might be better to die after all. I heard the General saying that our lives were forfeit, but that he had asked that we should be spared, and then about how wicked it was of the League of the Cities to have broken the treaty; I was wondering if it was any use my telling him that bad treaties ought to be broken, but just then Elxsente slipped forward and I had to catch him; he felt very hot and was breathing fast. The General came up to us and stooped over him; Elxsente threw his arms round my neck and held on tight with his face pressed into my shoulder; the General said, 'Don't be frightened,' and lifted his head quite gently; he asked how long he'd been like this, and I told him ten days, and said could we have some water for him. He asked if we had not had any, and I said yes, but that Elxsente had had his share and our share too, but he was all burnt up and always wanted more. He turned round to the Boar and the metal plates on his kilt swung against my face; he told him to get us water, and then felt Elxsente's head and hands, and told me he thought he would live. When the water came Elxsente let go of me with one hand and drank and looked up at the General, and Teffre drank, and then I drank; I've never tasted anything as good as that water; I felt quite different at once, and I would have spoken to the General to justify our Cities, only he went out.

That day we had dried figs with our bread, and in the evening they brought some milk for Elxsente. We heard how the General had marched up secretly and surprised and scattered our camp and relieved the town; a few days afterwards the Boar told us peace had been made; some of the Cities were given up to Rome, and the walls of Mireto had to be pulled down. Teffre and I talked it over; we wondered whether we ought to outlive the disgrace—*his* City was to pay tribute and have Rome for overlord—but finally we made up our minds to go on living for a little longer at least; we didn't quite know how to kill ourselves, and besides there was Elxsente; his City had to pay tribute too, but he didn't understand the shame of it, like we did.

By the time they let us out, Elxsente was much better, but we were none of us very strong. They tied us into a wagon; we sat on the bottom, out of the sun, and saw the tops of the trees that we passed under along the road, but not much else. The journey took three days, and then we stopped outside the walls of Rome. There was dust all over everything, dust in our hair and ears and eyelashes, dust caked on our hands and feet, white dust on the bread and fruit we ate. The wagon was drawn up on the inside of a square, and we sat on the edge trying to see what was happening; prisoners—our own men—were brought in under guard, formed up, and chained; of course we all looked hard to see if there was anyone we knew among them; often we thought we saw faces of friends, but they never were. Then one of my father's men was marched past and I shouted to him; he turned and called to me that my father had escaped, but he didn't know about my brother; still, that was something. There were women prisoners too, from the towns that had been taken, and armour and horses and gold cups from the altars of the Gods. Teffre saw one cartload from his own City and raged at being so helpless. And then Elxsente cried out and said he saw his cousin among the women, a white-faced girl with eyes swollen from tears and dust; we all called, but she didn't hear or heed, and Elxsente was terribly disappointed.

Then we were taken out of the wagon over to a heap of chains and one of the soldiers found light ones for us. Then we waited at the edge of the road till our turn came. The Roman soldiers went by first, crowned and singing; after them our prisoners, chained together; and more Romans; and trophies of swords and spears, and the pick of the cattle that had been taken; and more Romans; and a great line of women and children, and pictures of the battles, and ox-carts full of gold and silver, well guarded; and more Romans still, and more prisoners; and we were bitterly angry and sad. Then there was a place for us, and we joined the march with Roman soldiers in front of us and at each side. At first there was nothing but choking dust, until we got to the suburbs, where the streets had been watered, which kept the dust down and was pleasant to the feet. But then the crowds began, crowds of shouting enemies at the two edges of the road; they frightened me more than anything; we were so helpless and alone in the middle of them, and sometimes the noise would suddenly swell up into a roar all round us, and Elxsente would shrink up close to me; once or twice they threw things at us, but

nothing sharp enough to cut. A man who walked in front
of us kept on repeating in a shout that we were the hostages
from the Cities who were spared by order of the General
and that the rest were hung. He said it over and over again
like a corncrake: I would have given a lot to kill that man.
We must have had seven or eight miles to walk in the sun
at the pace of the slowest oxen; at first I looked about me
and whispered to the others from time to time and sang our
marching song under my breath, but later I was too tired
to do anything but stumble along with my head down.
My hands were chained behind my back so that I couldn't
even wipe the sweat off my forehead or the dust out of my
eyes. About half-way Teffre cut his foot on a sharp stone
and fell, but one of the guards picked him up and helped
him along. I was miserable about Elxsente; he wasn't well
yet and the sun was burning on our heads; he knew he must
go through the day without whimpering for the honour of
his City, and he did it well, but I could feel how much it
was costing him and I could do nothing to help him; I was
thankful when the soldier on his side said, 'I've a child of
my own', and took him on to his shoulder for part of the
way. The day seemed endless, but suddenly we were
halted in a great square place where someone was speaking
from the top of a flight of steps. I saw the General a long
way off, wearing a laurel wreath and a purple robe, but I
was too tired to see much; all those great white buildings
were swimming in the heat and there wasn't a breath of
wind to blow away the smell, that seemed everywhere, of
leather and onions, and the hot crowd.

When the Triumph was over and our chains were taken
off, we were locked up in a little barred room, a prison of

some sort, with straw on the flag-stones. We lay there, thankful for the dark and quiet, and slept like the dead all night. The first day a woman, who seemed too dazed to speak, brought us food; the second day another woman brought it; she was Elxsente's cousin. He rushed up to her, with, 'Where's mother?' and she burst into tears and put her arms round him. She had seen his father dead of wounds and knew his mother and baby sister were burned in a house with some other women who'd tried to escape from the soldiers. But she could hardly speak about it; something terrible must have happened to her too; and she mightn't stay with us. Elxsente cried all that day, and even while he slept he was sobbing and calling, 'Mother, mother'; I couldn't bear it, I put my hands over my ears so as not to hear, but I knew it was going on all the time and I couldn't sleep at all. Teffre was very much upset; he seemed to have thought that when it was all over he could go back to the old life, but this showed him that he couldn't; perhaps it was lucky for him that his mother was dead years before. Mireto had not been sacked, so my mother and sisters should have been safe, and I knew my father had escaped, but my brother might be killed or anything; and besides, I was the oldest and I realized it all better: how this was the end of the League of the Cities, our Gods were powerless, and our hope and honour in ashes.

The next morning we were taken away again; we were used to obeying orders now. An old soldier with a black beard was in charge of us; he wouldn't answer questions or let us talk among ourselves much. As we went through the streets a woman recognized us and threw a dead rat: it

hit Elxsente; but I was glad it wasn't a brick. We had a
long way to walk (though we got a lift for a few miles on
a wagon that was leaving the town empty), first along one
of the big main ways that went out between gardened
houses and under arches, right into the country, and then
along a lane with deep ruts, beside vineyards and cornfields;
it was past noon when we came to a long low house with
a walled garden where there were pomegranate trees.
There was no one to be seen, and the soldier stopped, sat
down on the bottom step of the ones that led up to the
house door, and ate bread and onions. We sat on the
ground beside him and waited, and the afternoon got
hotter and hotter; we were all very tired. We'd had nothing to eat since early that morning—we hoped the soldier
would give us something, but he didn't, and of course we
couldn't ask. Teffre was complaining of his foot, which
was badly swollen: I tied it up with fresh grass and a strip
from my own tunic. Elxsente was crying all the time,
quite hopelessly; his face was streaked with dirt and tears,
and his hair was tangled into grey knots all over his head.
I was unhappy enough myself; I tried to tell them stories,
but that reminded us of home and made it all worse.
Elxsente put his head down on my knee, and I felt his hot
little face, wet against my skin. Teffre cried every time he
moved his foot, and I was near it myself, but I thought of
our being among the enemy and that we must show we
were men. Still nobody came; sometimes we heard a cock
crowing behind the house, and once a reaper passed
through the trees in front of us with a sickle under his arm,
but he never looked our way.

Then we heard voices inside the house and a lady came

out on to the steps, with a maid carrying a basket behind
her. The soldier saluted and spoke to her; she was all in
blue, with the western sun on her face and hair. She ran
down the steps and saw us. 'Oh,' she said, 'oh—you children! You poor children!' and in a moment she was beside
me and had gathered Elxsente up into her arms; he lay
there limp with his eyes half-shut, still crying. 'Have you
been here all day,' she asked, 'with nothing to eat?' I
nodded and she called up to the maid to bring food and
drink quickly. I was glad to see how angry she was with
the soldier; she sent him away and sat down on the steps
with Elxsente on her knee, sobbing a little less. The maid
brought milk and barley cakes and pears and grapes; we
ate everything, and she fed Elxsente herself. Then the
General came round from the other side of the garden; I
knew him at once, though he was wearing a woollen tunic
and sandals instead of armour; the bailiff (though we didn't
know who he was till afterwards) was at his side. I stood
up, and his wife stood up holding Elxsente to her breast.

He looked at us kindly enough and told the bailiff to take
Teffre and me down to the pool to wash. We went with
him, Teffre limping badly; it was a broad, shallow, stone
basin, with sunflowers growing round it. We stripped and
went in and washed off layers and layers of dust and sweat,
and swam among the lily-pads till he told us to come out.
They brought us clean clothes and we put them on with
our hair dripping; he took us back to the house, to a clean,
light room with blankets spread on the floor for us, and
Teffre sat on a table while someone bandaged his foot properly. Then Elxsente came in and told us how the women
of the house had washed him and dressed him and been

kind to him, and he lay down on the blankets and I covered him, and he went to sleep almost at once. Then the General sent for me; he was sitting alone in a tall chair, with candles behind him. He asked me if I thought we should be ransomed; I said I believed Teffre and I would be, but that Elxsente's father and mother were killed, so I couldn't tell about him. He sent me away, and the mistress met me in the hall and asked if Elxsente was asleep.

The next day we were left alone most of the time, to eat and rest, but after that, when Teffre's foot was better, we were given work to do about the farm and garden, under the bailiff; it wasn't hard—getting in the grapes and apples, feeding the geese, driving the cows home, and so on. Elxsente got well wonderfully quickly, and forgot about his mother for hours together; the mistress petted him a lot and the General spoke to him whenever he saw him.

But the weeks went on and the autumn was going; there were frosts at night; once round the pond and out was as far as we cared to swim. But none of us heard anything from our homes. And then one day the General sent for Teffre to tell him he'd been ransomed, and his uncle was waiting to take him away. In an hour he'd said goodbye to us and was gone; I've never seen him since. Of course Elxsente and I were glad for his sake, but it made me wonder what was going to happen to me; I thought of all sorts of things; perhaps the soldier might have been wrong about my father; perhaps he was dead and my brother was dead, and all our money was gone; perhaps I should never see Mireto and my mother and our house again. Everyone was good to us, but of course we were no more free than any of the slaves, and I didn't like to think of all my life being like that. At one time I thought of running away, but I should probably have been caught, and anyhow I should have had to leave Elxsente; I had a plan that my father should ransom him too and he should come back and live with us and be my little brother, now that he had no one of his own kin left. We used to talk about that in the evenings.

But it was winter now. We were busy pruning the vines and fruit trees; Elxsente worked with me, but of course I had longer hours and did more. After it was dark the mistress used often to have us in and we sat with them, making withy plaits, while the General talked about farming and wild beasts and told us all his adventures. Sometimes he talked about Rome, things she had done in the past, things he said she would do in the future. I thought about Mireto and said nothing, but Elxsente seemed to believe it. We worshipped with them too: the country Gods are the same all the world over. Sometimes we went out after wolves and once I was in the thick of it, when either a hound or the wolf bit me in the arm. Looking back on it all now it seems such a waste of time that I didn't really enjoy it; but then I didn't know what had happened at home.

One day I was coming up to the house with my pruning knife and a great bundle of prunings to burn; Elxsente had gone in, but I had stayed to finish the row, and it was nearly dark; I heard hoofs behind me, turned, and there was my father! I threw down the bundle and ran to him, and he was off his horse and had me in his arms, all in a moment. The horse grazed by the roadside and we talked. Of course I asked first about mother and everyone. 'My little son,' he said, 'you didn't hear all this long time! All's well at home, but you know I'd spent all the money we had in arming my men. There was nothing left, and I had all I could do to raise enough to buy you both back. Did you know your brother was taken prisoner during the siege? I couldn't find him for months; he had been sold as a slave in the Roman market, and I bought him back first: he was having a bad time. But I thought you would be well treated here—they've not been unkind to you, son?' He looked at the bundle of wood, and then at the bound place on my arm where I'd had the wolf-bite. I told him they'd all been kind and what sort of life it was; he put me up on his horse—it was fine to be in the saddle again—with the prunings behind, and we went up to the house. The General met my father and took him in, and I led the horse round to the stables and bedded him down.

When I came in they'd settled my ransom, and father said we should go home the next day. I was so happy I could hardly think, and then, with a jump, I remembered Elxsente. 'Oh, father,' I said, 'can't you buy back my friend too? He's got no one left, and I told him I'd take him home with me.' Father looked miserable and said he couldn't—I found out afterwards how hard the ransom money had been to come by—but that he'd try to later, for the honour of the Cities. But the General said, 'I don't want to have Elxsente ransomed; I've another plan for him; call him and we'll see.' He came in, and the mistress with him; he ran over to me and took my hands: 'Oh, you're going,' he said, 'you're going back to your mother and I shall be left all alone!' But the General leaned forward, saying, 'Elxsente, you know I've no children of my own. Will you come and live with me always, and be my

E

son?' and the mistress spoke softly to him: 'Stay with us, dear.' And Elxsente looked at them and looked at me and then looked down on the floor, wondering. And I said, 'Think of your City, Elxsente! Don't put yourself into the hands of the enemy!' and he said to me, 'Would it be very wrong to stay? I think I'd like to stay'. I would have spoken, but my father stopped me and spoke himself: 'You know that I'm of the Cities, child, on your side; so you can trust me; and I advise you to stay.' Then Elxsente went over to the mistress and put his arms round her neck, and she and the General kissed him, and called him son. And then the General gave back the ransom money to my father and said to me that while there was peace I should always be welcome in his house.

The next day father and I set out for home. Elxsente came with us as far as the main road, and there we said our good-byes. Elxsente went back to the house, and father and I struck out over the hills for Mireto. We were back within the week and everything was right again. I found I hadn't mended my pony's bridle, but my brother had done it for me after he came home.

THE ENTHUSIASTIC PRISONER

The author of this story is an Australian farmer. During the Second World War, at a time of a great shortage of labour, he employed Italian prisoners of war on his sheep and wheat farm in New South Wales. It was from his knowledge of these Italians that he wrote the following story.

HENRY HOLDEN decided to get an Italian prisoner of war after he had seen several at work on Esmond's farm. Esmond was building a shed, and it was beautiful to see how they ran to get the things he needed, how they rushed to carry anything he picked up, and how they seemed to take it for granted that they were there to do all the heavy work while the boss gave the orders.

When the captain in charge of the P.W.C.C. had a preliminary look over Henry's place he tactlessly asked him if he was an invalid; he saw so few signs of work being done and so many of neglect. He wasn't at all keen on letting Henry have a P.W.; he didn't think he was the type to handle them successfully, but, on the other hand, he was eager to get his 'hundred'.

When the P.W. arrived, Henry was decidedly disappointed with him at first sight. He did not look obliging and polite; he didn't even look like an Italian. He had a tremendous amount of fuzzy brown hair; his eyebrows were so large and dense they nearly surrounded his eyes, and thick hair grew all round his neck and jutted out of his ears. His small, bright eyes glinted sharply from among all the hair; not at all like the large, soft and servile eyes of the Italians at Esmond's. In fact he reminded Henry of a big brown bear, with his air of having great physical strength and tremendous determination. When the military truck drove away Henry had an uncomfortable feeling of having let himself in for something.

He directed Pietro to his room, and while he was settling in, tried hurriedly to work out a plan of what to do with him. There was, of course, plenty of work to do, but it wasn't so easy to start a man who didn't understand English, or know Australian farms. In a few minutes Pietro appeared.

'Worrk,' he said, briefly and determinedly.

Henry abandoned his half-formed plan to let him have the first half of the day off to get settled. Getting quite panicky, he thought of a number of jobs, only to realize he didn't have the necessary materials. In desperation he decided to repair a fence. He pointed to the fence, and to some tools and tried to explain to Pietro.

'Unnerstan, reparare,' said Pietro.

Pietro picked up the shovel and pick, and started hunting for a 'leva'. Henry soon realized that he meant a crowbar, but he couldn't remember where his was. Pietro looked at him in astonished reproval. When they started off, Pietro carrying all the heavy tools while Henry carried the wire strainer, Henry felt better, though he was sure that Esmond's men would have offered to carry the wire strainer too.

They did little good with the fence although Pietro was obviously eager to work. It really needed a lot of new posts and wires, and Henry had neither. They tightened what wires were there and braced and stayed some of the key posts in a makeshift manner. Pietro liked the wire strainer, apparently he had never seen one before and he was greatly intrigued with the way it worked.

'Very ni, very ni,' he said.

But when they were going home for dinner he glanced disapprovingly at the propped-up posts.

'No good, no good,' he said.

Henry usually had a nap after dinner, which lasted well into the afternoon if the day happened to be warm. But Pietro apparently didn't know about 'dinner hours'. He waited outside the door for a while, then knocked and said, quite politely but very firmly, 'Worrk'.

Henry went out and remembered the wood-heap. It cheered him immensely. He had recently brought in a load and it would take Pietro several days to chop it up. It would be a great stand-by. Pietro could work there all the afternoon. He lay down while Pietro chopped with great vigour, but he could not sleep or even relax properly because of his problem. His wife and children, too, kept asking him questions about Pietro; they were rather awed by him.

He heard the rumble of the wheelbarrow on the veranda several times, and sounds of cut wood being tipped out. Then Pietro knocked on the door. He pointed to a great pile of wood and said, 'sufficiente?'

'No, not sufficient,' said Henry, 'chop more.'

Pietro looked at him with a blank expression.

'No unnerstan,' he said, and before Henry could work out another way of expressing himself, he inquired, 'Sufficiente one day? Two day? Tre day?'

'Tre day,' Henry admitted reluctantly.

Pietro smiled broadly and looked surprisingly pleasant as he did so. 'Plenty sufficiente,' he said, closing the argument.

Henry went and got his hat. He could hear the wind banging a loose sheet of iron on the roof of the machinery shed. They would begin by nailing it down. But when they got on the roof Pietro discovered that half the sheets were loose. Henry gave him nails and directed him to fasten down the flapping sheets. But Pietro was hunting round for causes. He discovered that the rafters were rotting, and demonstrated it by giving one a hard hit with the hammer. It split from end to end, and a couple of sheets immediately blew off the roof.

They spent the afternoon cutting trees in the scrub and trimming them for rafters, though nothing was farther from Henry's intention and inclination. He cut down a few little trees while Pietro cut a lot of big ones. Pietro always took the heavier end when they loaded the rails, but even so Henry became exhausted. Round about four o'clock he decided to go home.

'Sufficient,' he said.

Pietro consulted a diagram he had made.

'No sufficiente,' he said. 'Encora four.'

They went on working.

At tea that night Pietro met all the family. There was a flapper daughter, three younger boys, and a baby. He was particularly interested in the baby. He made some queer foreign noises at it, and to everyone's surprise it showed unmistakable signs of affection for him. He asked Mrs Holden if it was breast-fed, and when she told him, in some

Henry became exhausted

confusion, that it was not, he wanted to know why. Then he gave her detailed and intimate directions, mainly by signs, about how to ensure an abundant flow for the next baby. The flapper daughter half smothered a lot of embarrassed giggles, and the boys nearly 'busted' trying not to laugh. Henry felt that he ought to reprimand Pietro for his indelicacy, but didn't know how he could make him understand.

The next day Henry felt stiff and sore. He decided to relax, but Pietro kept calling him on to the roof; sometimes for advice, but mostly to help him in fitting rafters which were too big to be 'poseeble solo'.

They finished re-roofing the shed by the week-end. Pietro wanted to know if they would cut some fence-posts next week to repair the fences. Henry thought of how he would suffer if he had to work on the other end of a cross-cut-saw with a tireless bear like Pietro. He said, 'No, some other work.'

But he didn't like the way Pietro looked at him, so he decided to hide the crosscut-saw.

On Sunday Esmond's Italians came to visit Pietro. They must have told him all about what was going on at their place, because on Monday morning Pietro wanted to know why Henry was not preparing his soil for his crops, like Mr Esmond. Henry looked a bit guilty, then he tried to explain that he used different methods from Esmond's. Pietro was not satisfied.

'Mr Esmond good resultare? No good resultare?'

Henry had to admit that Esmond's results were good. He also had to confess that his own results were often bad.

'Provare similar Mr Esmond,' Pietro suggested enthusiastically. 'Poseeble very good oat, very good weet.'

'Tractor broken,' said Henry. He was always overwhelmed by a feeling of hopeless apathy in the autumn, and he couldn't face the strain of all the preparations necessary for his worn-out plant.

'Me look?' asked Pietro, and was off before Henry could say anything to the contrary.

Pietro had a thorough look over the tractor and scarifier. He made a list of all the new parts needed, which he laboriously translated into English with the help of his little dictionary. He explained that he was not a mechanic, but he had had a lot of experience with military vehicles. He suggested that Henry go to town and get the necessary parts, and Henry went, glad to get away from the responsibility of Pietro for an afternoon.

While Henry was away Pietro 'polished' the tool-shed and the farmyard. When Henry came home, rather late in the evening, and somewhat the worse for wine, he thought he had come to the wrong farm until Pietro came out of his room and carried his parcels for him. He was in an exalted mood and gave Pietro an orange for his services. But Pietro spoiled the effect by telling him of several things he had forgotten to bring.

At the table that night Pietro objected to Mrs Holden giving the baby honey to stop it crying.

'No good, 'oni, no good,' he said.

But she continued to exercise the lawful rights of a mother. Suddenly the baby vomited. Pietro made an angry noise, jumped up and put the honey away in the cupboard.

'No good, no good,' he said, so emphatically that she was startled and impressed.

Henry found that he couldn't tell Pietro much about overhauling farm machines. He stood by to tell him where tools, parts and materials were kept; frequently he found it easier to get them than to explain; sometimes when Pietro was held up and impatient Henry found himself running just like one of Esmond's Italians, until he remembered his dignity as a 'padrone'. They had an auspicious rain when everything was ready, and Henry's land was never worked into better condition.

The tractor ran very well. Pietro assumed a jealous control of it and appeared to be very happy on it no matter how long he worked. The arrangement suited Henry extremely well. He felt free for the first time since his prisoner arrived. He had plenty of time to turn over all the vague plans he had in his head.

When Pietro finished working the land he suggested again that they cut some fence posts. But Henry was ready with his own plan. Pietro was to paint the house. Pietro agreed heartily; the house certainly needed painting. They went to have a good look at the walls. Not only had the paint peeled off, but much of the plaster was cracked and loose.

'No good paint,' said Pietro. 'Prima plaster.'

But the thought of all the work and expense involved in plastering horrified Henry. He said authoritatively, 'Paint sufficient.' And he got a trowel and demonstrated how the rough plaster could be smoothed off sufficiently. He handed the trowel to Pietro, who made what appeared to be a similar movement. But the result was vastly different, at least a wheelbarrow-load of plaster fell off the wall.

'Plenty similar,' he said, and knocked off another square yard with a flick of his wrist. Henry gave in.

Henry was kept very busy mixing the plaster and carrying it to Pietro. It had to be mixed in small lots and applied immediately, Pietro said, otherwise it would fall off just like the previous coat.

When it was finished Henry brought out the paint. Pietro was very interested in the 'colore'. But when he discovered that it was to be a drab, uniform stone-colour all his eagerness vanished.

'No good, no good,' he said, 'similar dirt.'

He wouldn't take the brush when Henry offered it to him.

'Brush no good,' he said. 'Troppo old.'

Henry tried the brush and had to admit it was worn out. He decided to go to town and get a new one. Pietro wanted to go too; to get his hair cut. Henry left him at the Control Centre and went to do his shopping. When he walked into the general store, where he did most of his business, he had an uneasy feeling that he was being followed. He turned and saw Pietro carrying the two big tins of stone-coloured paint. He had that brown-bear look about him which Henry hadn't liked the first time he saw him.

The manager of the hardware came up to them. He saw by the look in Henry's eye that he wasn't sure of himself, so he turned to Pietro, who appeared to know exactly what he wanted. Pietro held up the tins.

'Colore no good,' he said.

The manager remembered having advised Henry against a uniform drab colour, and immediately set out to help

Pietro. He quite ignored Henry's somewhat indistinct, 'No, it's all right. I'll keep it.'

He showed Pietro a colour card and he selected a very light cream, a bright blue and a black.

'One big cream, one little blue, one little little nero,' he said.

The manager was, as he would have said, intrigued. He tried to discover what design Pietro had in mind, and Pietro demonstrated as best he could, attracting a lot of attention from other shoppers, who began to gather round. Henry became most uncomfortable.

'I won't have it at any price,' he protested, 'everyone who goes past will die laughing.'

'Ah, garn!' said a big voice from the back. 'Let him have a go. It couldn't look any worse than it's looked for the last twenty years.'

Then a couple of ladies joined in.

'How interesting!' said one. 'The Italians are so artistic, aren't they?'

The other one said, 'I remember seeing the adorable Italian cottages painted just like that; you must let us come and see it, Mr Holden.' She happened to be the wife of Henry's long-suffering mortgagee, and her word carried some weight with him. Quite a number of others voiced favourable opinions before Henry and Pietro carried out their cream, blue and black paint.

Pietro took endless pains over the painting, and all the time he was at it Henry felt resentful, despite the fact that many people came and admired it. He comforted himself by compiling a long list of heavy jobs Pietro would have to do when he was finished. He had the interpreter prepare a translation so that there would be no 'no unnerstan' business, and when at length the house was finished he gave Pietro a week's programme, consisting mainly of firewood carting and post-hole digging.

But that day it rained; a splendid soaking rain, and during the night it cleared. Henry was wakened early in the morning by the roar of the tractor starting. He was puzzled and rather annoyed; Pietro was up to something. Then he realized that Pietro had taken it upon himself to make the all-important decision of the year—that the time was right to start sowing the wheat.

Henry thought with some indignation of the programme he had given Pietro, but he also realized that it was much more important to get the wheat sown while the soil was moist. He lay thinking for a long time of ways in which he could reassert himself, and all the time he heard the noise of Pietro's preparations. He stayed there because he always hated the worry of working out the proportions of wheat and fertilizer, and adjusting the machines accordingly, and all the other important details necessary for a successful sowing season. When he finally went out, Pietro hurried up to him, his face aglow with enthusiasm.

'Oh, rain very nice,' he said. 'Terra very nice. Poseeble very good weet this year, similar Mr Esmond.'

He pointed to the tractor hitched to the sowing combine and the farm cart loaded with supplies of seed, fertilizer and tractor fuel.

'After brekfus me take trattore and wheat machine. You bring carro; allora we commence before Guiseppe and Leonardo on farm Mr Esmond.'

'O.K., Pietro,' said Henry.

HER FIRST BALL

This story was published in 1922; it recalls a girlhood in New Zealand even longer ago. Today girls do not 'put up their hair' before they go to their first dance; nor do they carry fans. 'Darling little pink-and-silver programmes with pink pencils and fluffy tassels' have gone for ever, and so have 'the poor old dears'—the mothers who sat on the platform watching their daughters dance—'the chaperones in dark dresses, smiling rather foolishly'.

Yet the excitement of a girl's first ball remains.

EXACTLY WHEN the ball began Leila would have found it hard to say. Perhaps her first real partner was the cab. It did not matter that she shared the cab with the Sheridan girls and their brother. She sat back in her own little corner of it, and the bolster on which her hand rested felt like the sleeve of an unknown young man's dress suit; and away they bowled, past waltzing lamp-posts and houses and fences and trees.

'Have you really never been to a ball before, Leila? But, my child, how too weird——' cried the Sheridan girls.

'Our nearest neighbour was fifteen miles,' said Leila softly, gently opening and shutting her fan.

Oh dear, how hard it was to be indifferent like the others! She tried not to smile too much; she tried not to care. But every single thing was so new and exciting. Meg's tuberoses, Jose's long loop of amber, Laura's little dark head, pushing above her white fur like a flower through snow. She would remember for ever. It even gave her a pang to see her cousin Laurie throw away the wisps of tissue paper he pulled from the fastenings of his new gloves. She would like to have kept those wisps as a keepsake, as a remembrance. Laurie leaned forward and put his hand on Laura's knee.

'Look here, darling,' he said. 'The third and the ninth as usual. Twig?'

Oh, how marvellous to have a brother! In her excitement Leila felt that if there had been time, if it hadn't been impossible, she couldn't have helped crying because she was an only child and no brother had ever said 'Twig?' to her; no sister would ever say, as Meg said to Jose that moment, 'I've never known your hair go up more successfully than it has tonight.'

But, of course, there was no time. They were at the drill hall already; there were cabs in front of them and cabs behind. The road was bright on either side with moving fanlike lights, and on the pavement gay couples seemed to float through the air; little satin shoes chased each other like birds.

'Hold on to me, Leila; you'll get lost,' said Laura.

'Come on, girls, let's make a dash for it,' said Laurie.

Leila put two fingers on Laura's pink velvet cloak, and they were somehow lifted past the big golden lantern, carried along the passage, and pushed into the little room marked 'Ladies'. Here the crowd was so great there was hardly space to take off their things; the noise was deafening. Two benches on either side were stacked high with wraps. Two old women in white aprons ran up and down tossing fresh armfuls. And everybody was pressing forward trying to get at the little dressing-table and mirror at the far end.

A great quivering jet of gas lighted the ladies' room. It couldn't wait; it was dancing already. When the door opened again and there came a burst of tuning from the drill hall, it leaped almost to the ceiling.

Dark girls, fair girls were patting their hair, tying ribbons again, tucking handkerchiefs down the fronts of their bodices, smoothing marble-white gloves. And because they were all laughing it seemed to Leila that they were all lovely.

'Aren't there any invisible hairpins?' cried a voice. 'How most extraordinary! I can't see a single invisible hairpin.'

'Powder my back, there's a darling,' cried someone else.

'But I must have a needle and cotton. I've torn simply miles and miles of the frill,' wailed a third.

Then, 'Pass them along, pass them along!' The straw basket of programmes was tossed from arm to arm. Darling little pink-and-silver programmes, with pink pencils and fluffy tassels. Leila's fingers shook as she took one out of the basket. She wanted to ask someone, 'Am I meant to have one too?' but she had just time to read: 'Waltz 3. *Two, Two in a Canoe*. Polka 4. *Making the Feathers Fly*,' when Meg cried, 'Ready, Leila?' and they pressed their way through the crush in the passage towards the big double doors of the drill hall.

Dancing had not begun yet, but the band had stopped tuning, and the noise was so great it seemed that when it did begin to play it would never be heard. Leila, pressing close to Meg, looking over Meg's shoulder, felt that even the little quivering coloured flags strung across the ceiling were talking. She quite forgot to be shy; she forgot how in the middle of dressing she had sat down on the bed with one shoe off and one shoe on and begged her mother to ring up her cousins and say she couldn't go after all. And the rush of longing she had had to be sitting on the veranda of their forsaken up-country home, listening to the baby owls crying 'More pork' in the moonlight, was changed to a rush of joy so sweet that it was hard to bear alone. She clutched her fan, and, gazing at the gleaming, golden floor, the azaleas, the lanterns, the stage at one end with its red carpet and gilt chairs and the band in a corner, she thought breathlessly, 'How heavenly; how simply heavenly!'

All the girls stood grouped together at one side of the doors, the men at the other, and the chaperones in dark dresses, smiling rather foolishly, walked with little careful steps over the polished floor towards the stage.

'This is my little country cousin Leila. Be nice to her. Find her partners; she's under my wing,' said Meg going up to one girl after another.

Strange faces smiled at Leila—sweetly, vaguely. Strange voices answered, 'Of course, my dear.' But Leila felt the girls didn't really see her. They were looking towards the men. Why didn't the men begin? What were they waiting for? There they stood, smoothing their gloves, patting their glossy hair and smiling among themselves. Then, quite suddenly, as if they had only just made up their minds that that was what they had to do, the men came gliding over the parquet. There was a joyful flutter among the girls. A tall, fair man flew up to Meg, seized her

F

programme, scribbled something; Meg passed him on to Leila. 'May I have the pleasure?' He ducked and smiled. There came a dark man wearing an eyeglass, then cousin Laurie came with a friend, and Laura with a little freckled fellow whose tie was crooked. Then quite an old man— fat, with a big bald patch on his head—took her programme and murmured, 'Let me see, let me see!' And he was a long time comparing his programme, which looked black with names, with hers. It seemed to give him so much trouble that Leila was ashamed. 'Oh, please don't bother,' she said eagerly. But instead of replying the fat man wrote something, glanced at her again. 'Do I remember this bright little face?' he said softly. 'Is it known to me of yore?' At that moment the band began playing; the fat man disappeared. He was tossed away on a great wave of music that came flying over the gleaming floor, breaking the groups up into couples, scattering them, sending them spinning. . . .

Leila had learned to dance at boarding school. Every Saturday afternoon the boarders were hurried off to a little corrugated iron mission hall where Miss Eccles (of London) held her 'select' classes. But the difference between that dusty-smelling hall—with calico texts on the walls, the poor, terrified little woman in a brown velvet toque with rabbit's ears, thumping the cold piano, Miss Eccles poking the girls' feet with her long white wand—and this, was so tremendous that Leila was sure if her partner didn't come and she had to listen to that marvellous music and to watch the others sliding, gliding over the golden floor, she would die at least, or faint, or lift her arms and fly out of one of those dark windows that showed the stars.

'Ours, I think——' Someone bowed, smiled, and offered her his arm; she hadn't to die after all. Someone's hand pressed her waist, and she floated away like a flower that is tossed into a pool.

'Quite a good floor, isn't it?' drawled a faint voice close to her ear.

'I think it's most beautifully slippery,' said Leila.

'Pardon!' The faint voice sounded surprised. Leila said it again. And there was a tiny pause before the voice echoed, 'Oh, quite!' and she was swung round again.

He steered so beautifully. There was the great difference between dancing with girls and men, Leila decided. Girls banged into each other and stamped on each other's feet; the girl who was the gentleman always clutched you so.

The azaleas were separate flowers no longer; they were pink and white flags streaming by.

'Were you at the Bells' last week?' the voice came again. It sounded tired. Leila wondered whether she ought to ask him if he would like to stop.

'No, this is my first dance,' said she.

Her partner gave a little gasping laugh. 'Oh, I say,' he protested.

'Yes, it is really the first dance I've ever been to.' Leila was most fervent. It was such a relief to be able to tell somebody. 'You see, I've lived in the country all my life up till now . . .'

At that moment the music stopped and they went to sit on two chairs against the wall. Leila tucked her pink satin feet under and fanned herself, while she blissfully watched the other couples passing and disappearing through the swing doors.

'Enjoying yourself, Leila?' asked Jose, nodding her golden head.

Laura passed and gave her the faintest little wink; it made Leila wonder for a moment whether she was quite grown up after all. Certainly her partner did not say very much. He coughed, tucked his handkerchief away, pulled down his waistcoat, took a minute thread off his sleeve. But it didn't matter. Almost immediately the band started and her second partner seemed to spring from the ceiling.

'Floor's not bad,' said the new voice. Did one always begin with the floor? And then, 'Were you at the Neaves' on Tuesday?' And again Leila explained. Perhaps it was a little strange that her partners were not more interested. For it was thrilling. Her first ball! She was only at the beginning of everything. It seemed to her that she had never known what the night was like before. Up till now it had been dark, silent, beautiful very often—oh yes—but mournful somehow. Solemn. And now it would never be like that again—it had opened dazzling bright.

'Care for an ice?' said her partner. And they went through the swing doors, down the passage, to the supper-room. Her cheeks burned, she was fearfully thirsty. How sweet the ices looked on little glass plates and how cold the frosted spoon was, iced too! And when they came back to the hall there was the fat man waiting for her by the door. It gave her quite a shock again to see how old he was; he ought to have been on the stage with the fathers and mothers. And when Leila compared him with her other partners he looked shabby. His waistcoat was creased, there was a button off his glove, his coat looked as if it was dusty with French chalk.

'Come along, little lady,' said the fat man. He scarcely troubled to clasp her, and they moved away so gently, it was more like walking than dancing. But he said not a word about the floor. 'Your first dance, isn't it?' he murmured.

'How *did* you know?'

'Ah,' said the fat man, 'that's what it is to be old!' He wheezed faintly as he steered her past an awkward couple. 'You see, I've been doing this kind of thing for the last thirty years.'

'Thirty years?' cried Leila. Twelve years before she was born!

'It hardly bears thinking about, does it?' said the fat man gloomily. Leila looked at his bald head, and she felt quite sorry for him.

'I think it's marvellous to be still going on,' she said kindly.

'Kind little lady,' said the fat man, and he pressed her a little closer and hummed a bar of the waltz. 'Of course,' he said, 'you can't hope to last anything like as long as that. No-o,' said the fat man, 'long before that you'll be sitting up there on the stage, looking on, in your nice black velvet. And these pretty arms will have turned into little short fat ones, and you'll beat time with such a different kind of fan —a black ebony one.' The fat man seemed to shudder. 'And you'll smile away like the poor old dears up there, and point to your daughter, and tell the elderly lady next to you how some dreadful man tried to kiss her at the club ball. And your heart will ache, ache'—the fat man squeezed her closer still, as if he really was sorry for that poor heart—'because no one wants to kiss you now. And you'll say how unpleasant these polished floors are to walk on, how dangerous they are. Eh, Mademoiselle Twinkle-toes?' said the fat man softly.

Leila gave a light little laugh, but she did not feel like laughing. Was it—could it all be true? It sounded terribly true. Was this first ball only the beginning of her last ball, after all? At that the music seemed to change; it sounded sad, sad; it rose upon a great sigh. Oh, how quickly things changed! Why didn't happiness last for ever? For ever wasn't a bit too long.

'I want to stop,' she said in a breathless voice. The fat man led her to the door.

'No,' she said, 'I won't go outside. I won't sit down. I'll just stand here, thank you.' She leaned against the wall, tapping with her foot, pulling up her gloves and trying to smile. But deep inside her a little girl threw her pinafore over her head and sobbed. Why had he spoiled it all?

'I say, you know,' said the fat man, 'you mustn't take me seriously, little lady.'

'As if I should!' said Leila, tossing her small dark head and sucking her underlip. . . .

Again the couples paraded. The swing doors opened and shut. Now new music was given out by the band-master. But Leila didn't want to dance any more. She wanted to be home, or sitting on the veranda listening to those baby owls. When she looked through the dark windows at the stars they had long beams like wings . . .

But presently a soft, melting, ravishing tune began, and a young man with curly hair bowed before her. She would have to dance, out of politeness, until she could find Meg. Very stiffly she walked into the middle; very haughtily she

In one minute, in one turn, her feet glided, glided

put her hand on his sleeve. But in one minute, in one turn, her feet glided, glided. The lights, the azaleas, the dresses, the pink faces, the velvet chairs, all became one beautiful flying wheel. And when her next partner bumped her into the fat man and he said, 'Par*don*', she smiled at him more radiantly than ever. She didn't even recognize him again.

THE MAN OF THE HOUSE

The scene of this story is laid in south-west Ireland in the city of Cork.

As A KID I was as good as gold so long as I could concentrate. Concentration, that was always my trouble, in school and everywhere else. Once I was interrupted I was lost.

It was like that when the mother got the bad cough. I remember it well, waking in the morning and hearing it downstairs in the kitchen, and I knew there was something wrong. I dressed and went down. She was sitting in a little wickerwork chair in front of the fire, holding her side. She had made an attempt to light the fire but it had gone against her.

'What's wrong, mum?' I asked.

'The sticks were wet and the fire started me coughing,' she said, trying to smile though I could see she was doubled up with pain.

'I'll light the fire and you go back to bed,' I said.

'Ah, how can I, child?' she said. 'Sure, I have to go to my work.'

'You couldn't work like that,' I said. 'Go on up to bed and I'll bring you up your breakfast.'

It's a funny thing about women, the way they'll take orders from anything in trousers, even if 'tis only ten.

'If you could make a cup of tea for yourself, I'd be all

right in an hour or so,' she said and shuffled feebly towards
the stairs. I held her arm and she plonked down on the
bed. I knew then she must be feeling bad. I got more
sticks—she was so economical that she never used enough
sticks—and soon I had the fire roaring and the kettle on. I
made her toast as well; I was always a great believer in
buttered toast. I thought she looked at the cup of tea rather
doubtfully.

'Is that all right?' I asked.

'You wouldn't have a sup of boiling water left?' she
said.

''Tis too strong,' I agreed with a trace of disappointment
I tried to keep out of my voice. 'I'll pour half it away. I
can never remember about tea.'

'I hope you won't be late for school,' she said anxiously.

'I'm not going to school,' I said. 'I'll get you your tea
now and I'll do the shopping afterwards.'

I was rather proud of myself, the cool way I had said I
wasn't going to school and the mother's acceptance of it.
I washed up the breakfast things, then I washed myself and
went up with the shopping basket, a piece of paper and a
lead pencil.

'I'll do the messages now if you'll write them down,' I
said. 'Would I get the doctor?'

'Indeed,' said my mother anxiously, 'you'll do nothing
of the kind. He'd only want to send me to hospital. You
could call at the chemist and ask him to give you a good,
strong cough bottle.'

'Write it down,' I said, remembering my own weakness.
'If I haven't it written down I might forget it. And put
"strong" in big letters. What will I get for dinner? Eggs?'

Like the doctor, that was only a bit of swank because eggs were the only thing I could cook, but mother told me to get sausages as well in case she got up.

It was a lovely sunny morning, and on my way to the cross I had to pass the school. There was a steep hill opposite it and I stood there for a full ten minutes, staring. The schoolhouse and the sloping yard were like a picture except for the chorus of poor victims through the opened windows, and a glimpse of Danny Delaney's bald pate as he did sentry-go near the front door with his cane behind his back. That was grand. It was nice, too, chatting with the fellows in the shops and telling them about the mother's cough. I made it out a bit worse than it was, to make a good story of it, and partly in hopes that she'd be up when I got home the way we could have sausages for dinner. I hated boiled eggs.

When I got in I rushed upstairs at once and found Minnie Ryan with her. Minnie was a middle-aged woman, gossipy and pious but very knowledgeable.

'How are you feeling now, mum?' I asked.

'I'm miles better,' she said with a smile, taking the cough bottle I had got her.

'She won't be able to get up today though,' Minnie said very firmly.

'I'll put on the kettle and make a cup of tea for you so,' I said.

'Wisha, I'll do that for you, child,' said Minnie at once.

'Ah, you needn't mind, Miss Ryan,' I said. 'I can manage all right.'

'Wisha, isn't he great?' I heard her say in a low voice as I went downstairs.

'Oh, as good as gold!' exclaimed my mother.

'Why then, there aren't many like him,' said Minnie with a sigh. 'The most of the children that's going now are more like savages than Christians.'

In the afternoon my mother wanted me to play but I wouldn't go far. I remembered my own weakness. I knew if once I went a certain distance from the house I should drift towards the Glen, with the barrack drill field perched on a chalky cliff above; the rifle-range below it, and below that again, the mill-pond and mill-stream running through a wooded gorge—the Rockies, Himalayas or Highlands according to your mood. Concentration, that was what I had to practise.

Evening fell; the street-lamps were lit and the paper-boy went crying up the road. I bought a paper, lit the lamp in the kitchen and the candle in the bedroom, and read to my mother from the police court news. I wasn't very quick about it because I was only at words of one syllable, but she didn't seem to mind that.

Later, Minnie Ryan came again and as she was going I went to the door with her.

'If she's not better in the morning I think I'd get the doctor to her,' she said, not looking at me at all.

'Why?' I asked in alarm. 'Do you think is she worse, Miss Ryan?'

'Ah, sha, no,' she said, giving her old shawl a tug, 'but I'd be frightened of the pneumonia.'

'But wouldn't he send her to hospital, Miss Ryan?'

'Ah, he might and he mightn't,' she said, leaving me in no doubt of what he'd do. 'But that inself, wouldn't it be better than neglecting it? If you had a drop of whiskey you could give it to her hot with a squeeze of lemon in it.'

'I'll get it,' I said at once.

The mother didn't want the whiskey, because of the expense, but the fear of the hospital and the pneumonia was strong on me and I wouldn't be put off. I had never been in a public-house before and the crowd inside frightened me.

'Hullo, my old flower,' said one tall man, grinning at me diabolically. 'It must be ten years since I seen you last. One minute now—wasn't it in South Africa?'

My pal, Bob Connell, told me how he once asked a drunk man for a half-crown, and the man gave it to him. I was always trying to work up courage to try the same thing, but I didn't feel like it just then.

'It was not,' I said. 'I want half a glass of whiskey for my mother.'

'Oh, the thundering ruffian!' said the man, clapping his hands. 'Pretending 'tis for his mother and he had to be carried home that night in Bloemfontein.'

'I had not,' I shouted on the verge of tears. 'And 'tis for my mother. She's sick.'

'Ah, let the child alone, Johnnie,' said the barmaid, and then I went off and got the lemon.

My mother fell asleep after drinking the hot whiskey, but somehow I couldn't rest. I was wondering how the man in the pub could have thought I was in South Africa, and blaming myself a lot for not asking him for a half-crown. A half-crown would be very handy if the mother was sick. When I did fall asleep I was wakened by her coughing, and when I went into her she was rambling in her speech. It frightened me more than anything that she didn't know me, and I lay awake in dread of what would happen if it really was pneumonia.

When she was no better in the morning the depression was terrible. After giving her her breakfast I went to Minnie Ryan.

'I'd get the doctor at once,' she said firmly.

To get the doctor I had to go first to the house of a Poor Law Guardian for a ticket to show we couldn't pay, and then to the dispensary. After that I had to rush back, get the house ready and prepare a basin of water, soap and towel for the doctor to wash his hands.

He didn't come until after dinner. He was a fat, loud-voiced man, and, like all the drunks of the medical profession, supposed to be 'the cleverest man in Cork if only he'd mind himself'. To judge from the way he looked he hadn't been minding himself much that morning.

'How are you going to get this now?' he growled, sitting on the edge of the bed with the prescription pad on his knee. 'The only place open is the North Dispensary.'

'I'll go, doctor,' I said at once.

''Tis a long way,' he said doubtfully. 'Do you know where it is?'

'I'll find it,' I said.

'Isn't he a great little chap?' he said to the mother.

'Oh, the best in the world, doctor,' she sighed. 'A daughter couldn't be better to me.'

'That's right,' he said. 'Look after your mother while you can; she'll be the best for you in the long run . . . We don't mind them when we have them,' he added to my mother, 'and then we spend the rest of our lives regretting it.'

I didn't think myself he could be a very good doctor, because, after all my trouble he never washed his hands, but I was relieved that he said nothing about the hospital. I went to the door with him to see him off.

'Sure, she won't have to go to hospital, doctor?' I said.

'Not with a good nurse like you to mind her,' he said, patting my shoulder and blowing his whiskey-breath in my face.

The road to the dispensary led first uphill through a thickly-populated poor locality as far as the barrack which was perched on the hill-top, and then descended between high walls till it suddenly almost disappeared in a stony pathway with red-brick corporation houses to one side, and on the other, a wide common with an astounding view of the city. The pathway dropped away to the bank of a little stream where a brewery stood, and from that, far beneath you, the opposite hillside, a murmuring honey-comb of houses whose noises came to you, dissociated and ghostlike, rose to the gently rounded top with a limestone spire and a purple sandstone tower rising out of it. It was so wide a view that it was never all lit up together; the sunlight wandered across it as across a prairie, picking out a line of roofs with a brightness like snow or delving into the depth of some dark street and outlining in shadow the figures of climbing carts and straining horses. I was full of noble ideas. I made up my mind that I'd spend the penny my mother had given me on a candle to the Blessed Virgin in the cathedral to make her better quick. I felt sure I'd get more value in a big church like that so close to heaven.

The dispensary was a sordid hallway with a bench to one

side and a window like a railway ticket office at the end. There was a little girl with a green plaid shawl about her shoulders sitting on the bench. She gave me a quick look and I saw that her eyes were green too. I knocked at the window and a seedy, angry-looking man opened it. Without listening to what I had to say he grabbed bottle and prescription from me and banged the shutter down again without a word. I waited a minute and then lifted my hand to knock a second time.

'You'll have to wait, little boy,' the girl said quickly.

'Why will I have to wait?' I asked.

'He have to make it up,' she explained. 'He might be half an hour. Sit down, can't you?'

'Where are you from?' she went on after I did. 'I live in Blarney Lane,' I told her, and then she asked me who the bottle was for.

'My mother,' I said.

'What's wrong with her?' asked the girl.

'She have a terrible cough,' said I.

'She might have consumption,' said the little girl. 'That's what my sister that died last year had. I'm waiting for a tonic for my other sister. She have to have tonics all the time. Is it nice where ye live?'

So I told her about the Glen, and she told me about the river out to Carrigrohane. It seemed to be a nicer place altogether than ours, the way she described it. She was a nice, talkative little girl and I never noticed the time till the shutter went up and a bottle was banged down on the counter.

'Dooley!' shouted the seedy man and the window shut again.

'That's for me,' said the little girl. 'Yours won't be ready for a long time yet. I'll wait for you.'

'I have a lop,' I said, showing her my penny. 'Boy, we'll be able to get a bag of sweets for that.'

I liked that little girl a lot. She restored my confidence. I knew now that I was exaggerating things and that the mother would be all right without any self-sacrifice on my part. We sat on the steps by the infirmary and ate the sweets. At the end of the lane was the limestone spire, all along it young trees overhung the high walls, and the sun, when it came out in hot golden blasts behind us, threw our linked shadows out on to the road.

'Give us a taste of your bottle, little boy,' she said.

'Can't you taste your own?' I replied suspiciously.

'Ah, mine is awful,' she said with a mournful shrug. 'Tonics is awful. Try it, if you like.'

I did, and hastily spat it out. Awful was the word for it. But after that, I couldn't do less than let her taste mine. She took a long swig out of it that alarmed me.

'That's grand!' she said enthusiastically. 'I love cough bottles. Try it yourself and see.'

I did, and saw that she was right about that too. It was very sweet and sticky, like treacle, only with more bite in it.

'Give us another,' she said, grabbing at it.

'I will not,' I said in alarm. ''Twill be all gone.'

'Ah, don't be an old miser,' she said scornfully, with a curious pout. 'You have gallons of it.'

And somehow I couldn't refuse her. My mother was far away, and I was swept from anchorage into an unfamiliar world of spires and towers, trees, steps and little girls with

G

red hair and green eyes. I worshipped that girl. We both took another swig and then I really began to panic.

'It's nearly all gone,' I said, beginning to snivel. 'What am I going to do now?'

'Finish it and say the cork fell out,' she replied as though it were the most natural thing in the world, and God forgive me, I believed her. We finished it between us, and then, gradually as I put down the empty bottle I remembered my mother sick and the Blessed Virgin slighted, and my heart sank. I had sacrificed both to a little girl, and she didn't even care for me. It was my cough bottle she was after all the time. Too late I saw her guile and burst into tears.

'What ails you?' she asked in astonishment.

'My mother is sick and you're after drinking her medicine, and now if she dies 'twill be my fault,' I said.

'Ah, don't be an old cry-baby!' she said contemptuously. 'You need only say that the cork fell out—'tis a thing that might happen to anyone.'

'And I promised the Blessed Virgin a candle, and I spent it all on sweets for you!' I screamed, and away with me up the road like a madman, holding the empty bottle. Now, I had only one refuge and hope—a miracle. I went into the cathedral to the shrine of the Blessed Virgin, and having told her about my fall, I promised her a candle with the very next penny I got if only she'd make my mother better by the time I got back. I looked at her face carefully in the candlelight and I thought she didn't look too cross. Then I crawled miserably back over the hill. All the light had gone out of the day, and the echoing hillside had become a

We finished it between us

vast alien, cruel world. As well as that I felt terrible sick after the cough bottle. It even crossed my mind that I might die myself. In one way it would be a great ease to me.

When I got home the silence of the kitchen and the sight of the empty grate showed me at once that the Blessed Virgin had let me down. The mother was still in bed. I couldn't bear it, and I began to howl.

'What is it at all, child?' my mother cried anxiously from upstairs.

'I lost the medicine,' I bellowed from the foot of the stairs and then dashed blindly up and buried my face in the bedclothes.

'Oh, wisha, wisha, wisha, if that's all that's a trouble to you, you poor misfortunate child!' she cried in relief, running her hand through my hair. 'Is anything the matter?' she added anxiously. 'You're very hot.'

'I drank the medicine,' I bellowed and then buried my face again.

'And if you did itself, what harm?' she murmured soothingly. 'You poor child! Going all that way by yourself, without a proper dinner or anything, and then to have your journey for nothing. Undress yourself now, and rest here for a while.'

She rose, put on her slippers and her overcoat and unlaced my boots while I sat on the bed. Even before she was finished I was fast asleep. I didn't see her dress herself or hear her go out, but some time later I felt a hand on my forehead and saw Minnie Ryan peering down at me, laughing.

'Arrah, 'tis nothing, woman,' she said lightly. 'He'll

sleep that off by morning. Aren't they the divil? The dear knows, Mrs Sullivan, 'tis you should be in bed.'

I knew. I knew it was her judgement on me; I was one of those that were more savages than Christians; I was no good as a nurse, no good as anything. I accepted it all. But when my mother came up with her paper and read it beside my bed, I felt I could afford to let them all despise me, because there was one who didn't. My prayer was answered. The miracle had happened.

AUGUST 2001—THE SETTLERS

*The planet Mars has long attracted the interest of astronomers.
Through their telescopes they can observe strange features on its
surface and odd changes of colouring, which suggest that on Mars,
as on Earth, shrubs blossom and leaf in springtime, and that
grass withers and grows brown in the heat of summer. At both
poles there is an ice cap which grows in size during winter and
melts at the edges in the Martian spring. Much of the surface
of the planet is an orange brown, as though it were arid desert,
and it is known that the climate of the planet, judged by the
Earth's standards, is extremely severe. On the Martian equator
temperatures rise to 86° Fahrenheit in the day time, but at dusk
they sink well below freezing point. Long circle markings have
been observed stretching across the globe. These are so regular
that some scientists have wondered whether they were not canals
cut by marvellously ingenious Martian engineers.*

*Mars is the only planet on which it is possible that animal life
exists. Yet the rigours of the climate, the sparsity of the vegeta-
tion, and, above all, the thinness of the atmosphere make life, as
we know it, very difficult to imagine. There is less oxygen in
the air above the Martian desert than there is on the top of Mount
Everest, and over most of the planet water is very scarce.*

*When the inter-planetary travellers of the future rocket their
way through the thirty-five million miles of space which separate
us from those unearthly orange plains, what kind of existence
will they find awaiting them? Gasping in the thin air for oxygen
with which to fill their lungs, what heroic tasks will the pioneer*

settlers not perform to make this planet a brave new world for our grandchildren?

THE MEN of Earth came to Mars.

They came because they were afraid or unafraid, because they were happy or unhappy, because they felt like Pilgrims or did not feel like Pilgrims. There was a reason for each man. They were leaving bad wives or bad jobs or bad towns; they were coming to find something or leave something or get something, to dig up something or bury something or leave something alone. They were coming with small dreams or large dreams or none at all. But a government finger pointed from the four-colour posters in many towns: THERE'S WORK FOR YOU IN THE SKY: SEE MARS! and the men shuffled forward, only a few at first, a double-score, for most men felt the great illness in them even before the rocket fired into space. And this disease was called The Loneliness, because when you saw your home town dwindle the size of your fist and then lemon-size and then pin-size and vanish in the fire-wake, you felt you had never been born, there was no town, you were nowhere, with space all around, nothing familiar, only other strange men. And when the state of Illinois, Iowa, Missouri, or Montana vanished into cloud seas, and, doubly, when the United States shrank to a misted island and the entire planet Earth became a muddy baseball tossed away, then you were alone, wandering in the meadows of space, on your way to a place you couldn't imagine.

So it was not unusual that the first men were few. The number grew steadily in proportion to the census of Earth

Men already on Mars. There was comfort in numbers.
But the first Lonely Ones had to stand by themselves. . .

DECEMBER 2001—THE GREEN MORNING

WHEN THE sun set he crouched by the path and cooked a
small supper and listened to the fire crack while he put the
food in his mouth and chewed thoughtfully. It had been
a day not unlike thirty others, with many neat holes dug
in the dawn hours, seeds dropped in, and water brought
from the bright canals. Now, with an iron weariness in
his slight body, he lay and watched the sky colour from
one darkness to another.

His name was Benjamin Driscoll, and he was thirty-one
years old. And the thing that he wanted was Mars grown
green and tall with trees and foliage, producing air, more
air, growing larger with each season; trees to cool the
towns in the boiling summer, trees to hold back the winter
winds. There were so many things a tree could do: add
colour, provide shade, drop fruit, or become a children's
playground, a whole sky universe to climb and hang from;
an architecture of food and pleasure, that was a tree. But
most of all the trees would distil an icy air for the lungs,
and a gentle rustling for the ear when you lay nights in
your snowy bed and were gentled to sleep by the sound.

He lay listening to the dark earth gather itself, waiting
for the sun, for the rains that hadn't come yet. His ear to
the ground, he could hear the feet of the years ahead moving at a distance, and he imagined the seeds he had placed
today sprouting up with green and taking hold on the sky,
pushing out branch after branch, until Mars was an afternoon forest, Mars was a shining orchard.

In the early morning, with the small sun lifting faintly among the folded hills, he would be up and finished with a smoky breakfast in a few minutes and, treading out the fire ashes, be on his way with knapsacks, testing, digging, placing seed or sprout, tamping lightly, watering, going on, whistling, looking at the clear sky brightening towards a warm noon.

'You need the air,' he told his night fire. The fire was a ruddy, lively companion that snapped back at you, that slept close by with drowsy pink eyes warm through the chilly night. 'We all need the air. It's a thin air here on Mars. You get tired too soon. It's like living in the Andes, in South America, high. You inhale and don't get anything. It doesn't satisfy.'

He felt his rib-case. In thirty days, how it had grown. To take in more air, they would all have to build their lungs. Or plant more trees.

'That's what I'm here for,' he said. The fire popped. 'In school they told a story about Johnny Appleseed walking across America planting apple-trees. Well, I'm doing more. I'm planting oaks, elms and maples, every kind of tree, aspens and deodars * and chestnuts. Instead of making just fruit for the stomach, I'm making air for the lungs. When those trees grow up some year, *think* of the oxygen they'll make!'

He remembered his arrival on Mars. Like a thousand others, he had gazed out upon a still morning and thought, How do I fit here? What will I do? Is there a job for me?

Then he had fainted.

* A kind of cedar tree.

Someone pushed a vial of ammonia to his nose and, coughing, he came round.

'You'll be all right,' said the doctor.

'What happened?'

'The air's pretty thin. Some can't take it. I think you'll have to go back to Earth.'

'No!' He sat up, and almost immediately felt his eyes darken and Mars revolve twice round under him. His nostrils dilated and he forced his lungs to drink in deep nothingnesses. 'I'll be all right. I've got to stay here!'

They let him lie gasping in horrid fish-like motions. And he thought, Air, air, air. They're sending me back because of air. And he turned his head to look across the Martian fields and hills. He brought them to focus, and the first thing he noticed was that there were no trees, no trees at all, as far as you could look in any direction. The land was down upon itself, a land of black loam, but nothing on it, not even grass. Air, he thought, the thin stuff whistling in his nostrils. Air, air. And on top of hills, or in their shadows, or even by little creeks, not a tree and not a single green blade of grass. Of course! He felt the answer came not from his mind, but his lungs and his throat. And the thought was like a sudden gust of pure oxygen, raising him up. Trees and grass. He looked down at his hands and turned them over. He would plant trees and grass. That would be his job, to fight against the very thing that might prevent his staying here. He would have a private horticultural war with Mars. There lay the old soil, and the plants of it so ancient they had worn themselves out. But what if new forms were introduced? Earth trees, great mimosas and weeping willows and mag-

nolias and magnificent eucalyptus. What then? There
was no guessing what mineral wealth hid in the soil, un-
tamed because the old ferns, flowers, bushes and trees had
tired themselves to death.

'Let me up!' he shouted. 'I've got to see the Co-
ordinator!'

He and the Co-ordinator had talked an entire morning
about things that grew and were green. It would be
months, if not years, before organized planting began. So
far, frosted food was brought from Earth in flying icicles;
a few community gardens were greening up in hydroponic
plants.*

'Meanwhile,' said the Co-ordinator, 'it's your job.
We'll get what seed we can for you, a little equipment.
Space on the rockets is mighty precious now. I'm afraid,
since these towns are mining communities, there won't be
much sympathy for your tree-planting . . .'

'But you'll let me do it?'

They let him do it. Provided with a single motor-cycle,
its bin full of rich seeds and sprouts, he had parked his
vehicle in the valley wilderness and struck out on foot over
the land.

That had been thirty days ago, and he had never glanced
back.

For looking back would have been sickening to the
heart. The weather was excessively dry; it was doubtful if
any seeds had sprouted yet. Perhaps his entire campaign,
his four weeks of bending and scooping were lost. He kept
his eyes only ahead of him, going on down this wide,

---

* Greenhouses in which plants are grown in water and chemicals
without the use of soil.

shallow valley under the sun, away from First Town, waiting for the rains to come.

Clouds were gathering over the dry mountains now as
he drew his blanket over his shoulders. Mars was a place
as unpredictable as time. He felt the baked hills simmering
down into frosty night, and he thought of the rich, inky
soil, a soil so black and shiny it almost crawled and stirred
in your fist, a rank soil from which might sprout gigantic
beanstalks from which, with bone-shaking concussion,
might drop screaming giants.

The fire fluttered into sleepy ash. The air tremored to
the distant roll of a cart-wheel. Thunder. A sudden odour
of water. Tonight, he thought, and put his hand out to
feel for rain. Tonight.

He awoke to a tap on his brow.

Water ran down his nose into his lips. Another drop hit
his eye, blurring it. Another splashed his chin.

The rain.

Raw, gentle, and easy, it mizzled out of the high air, a
special elixir, tasting of spells and stars and air, carrying a
peppery dust in it, and moving like a rare light sherry on
his tongue.

Rain.

He sat up. He let the blanket fall and his blue denim shirt
spot, while the rain took on more solid drops. The fire
looked as though an invisible animal were dancing on it,
crushing it, until it was angry smoke. The rain fell. The
great black lid of sky cracked in six powdery blue chips,
like a marvellous crackled glaze, and rushed down. He
saw ten billion rain crystals, hesitating long enough to be

photographed by the electrical display. Then darkness and water.

He was drenched to the skin, but he held his face up and let the water hit his eyelids, laughing. He clapped his hands together and stepped up and walked around his little camp, and it was one o'clock in the morning.

It rained steadily for two hours and then stopped. The stars came out, freshly washed and clearer than ever.

Changing into dry clothes from his cellophane pack, Mr Benjamin Driscoll lay down and went happily to sleep.

The sun rose slowly among the hills. It broke out upon the land quietly and wakened Mr Driscoll where he lay.

He waited a moment before rising. He had worked and waited a long hot month, and now, standing up, he turned at last and faced the direction from which he had come.

It was a green morning.

As far as he could see, the trees were standing up against the sky. Not one tree, not two, not a dozen, but the thousands he had planted in seed and sprout. And not little trees, no, not saplings, not little tender shoots, but great trees, huge trees, trees as tall as ten men, green and green and huge and round and full, trees shimmering their metallic leaves, trees whispering, trees in a line over hills, lemontrees, lime-trees, redwoods and mimosas and oaks and elms and aspens, cherry, maple, ash, apple, orange, eucalyptus, stung by a tumultuous rain, nourished by alien and magical soil and, even as he watched, throwing out new branches, popping open new buds.

'Impossible!' cried Mr Benjamin Driscoll.

But the valley and the morning were green.

And the air!

All about, like a moving current, a mountain river, came the new air, the oxygen blowing from the green trees. You could see it shimmer high in crystal billows. Oxygen, fresh, pure, green, cold oxygen turning the valley into a river delta. In a moment the town doors would flip wide, people would run through the new miracle of oxygen, sniffing, gusting in lungfuls of it, cheeks pinking with it, noses frozen with it, lungs revivified, hearts leaping, and worn bodies lifted into a dance.

Mr Benjamin Driscoll took one long deep drink of green water air and fainted.

Before he woke again five thousand new trees had climbed up into the yellow sun.

FEAR

The scene of this story is set in Western Australia, some eight hundred miles north of Perth, in an immense area known as the North West. Here the grassy plains are cut by water courses which run dry in winter except for occasional deep 'holes' or pools left in the sand. The river banks are lined with white-trunked eucalyptus trees, known as 'river-gums'. In summer the rains fall in bursts, and along the coast the countryside is sometimes ravaged by 'willy-willies' or cyclones.

The story is based on an incident that occurred more than eighty years ago, when the first white settlers were pushing out from the little town of Roebourne. At this time the wild Australian aborigines from the ranges were beginning to help the settlers. The men worked as stockmen on the first sheep farms, and the women, known by the native name of 'gins', helped the settlers' wives in the homesteads.

In this huge empty landscape on 'the rim of civilization', ignorant of each others' fears and brutalities, Europeans and natives were meeting often for the first time.

THE WOMAN stood in the doorway of her wood-and-iron house and looked across to the big shed. If anything, the shed appeared rather better finished than the house. But they were neither of them much; the buildings had only been there a year or two—set back a little from the creek, where the river-gums, as befitted the only trees for miles, smirked at their reflections in a dark pool—set back right on the edge of the ranges, on the very rim of civilization.

The slanting afternoon sun made the spiky, prickly tufts of spinifex grass look soft, luxurious; then spent its golden virtue in a riot of rainbow colour over on the ironstone ridge. And the dry, aromatic smell of an uninhabited land rose fragrant to the nostrils.

Behind the house, in the brush lean-to serving as kitchen —it was cooler that way and kept the flies from the house— the woman could hear Edie and Sam at play with pots and cans. She would have to stop them—too costly and difficult to get if small hands should do damage. And they'd be getting into the store-cupboard next—Sam was a terror for sugar, just like the natives! Baby would be awake in a few minutes, too; he was regular as a clock for his feed.

Yet she continued to stand there, staring across at the shed. She was feeling restless; had she not been a woman of great sense and fortitude, she would have called herself nervous.

The sunlight streamed without mercy on her well-worn print dress with its boned bodice and yards of skirt; but it caressed lightly a young face long since drained of colour, tanned to a golden brown. The light had drawn early lines round a pair of blue eyes, too; she was for ever running out, hatless, into the glare after the children.

All round about the few scattered buildings roamed her blue eyes. Except for little noises from the children, and the caw-cawing of crows sailing over the killing pen, an unearthly silence wrapped the place. Not a native in sight. The kitchen gins had padded off to their noon camp the

moment washing-up was over. Most afternoons she could
stand and listen to the tapping of sticks or a drowsy corroboree * chant. But today everything was silent. She
imagined it must have been the silence that had brought
her out.

Where were little Johnnie, and that Lloyd?

She didn't like Lloyd. She had told John so, many a
time. But her husband just said men were difficult to get;
Lloyd was all right, a good stockman and all that. But she
didn't trust the fellow; he was altogether too rough on the
natives. John himself could be brutal enough at times,
but he was always just; the boys respected the boss, liked
him—his kind of brutality was their own, and seen only
when the isolation of the place rendered a firm hand
advisable. But that Lloyd! She could never forget seeing
him set the dogs on to the gins one day, so the poor
wretches ran screaming to the trees and scaled them like
cats. Horrible, it had been. And Lloyd had laughed fit to
kill himself. Pity he hadn't! She had told John. That time
he had spoken to the man, said such a thing must not happen again. And it hadn't.

All the same, she did wish it had not been necessary for
John to go into the port to meet their first mob of sheep, to
leave her like this, alone with the children and Lloyd.

The man she was thinking about came suddenly round
the shed, little Johnnie at his heels. The small boy staggered
along under the weight of a saddle; the man carried a knot
of twine. The mother's anger rose. Just like him! There

* A corroboree is a native dance, performed to the tapping of sticks
and songs. The songs have a distinctive rhythm and are sung nearly
every evening as the natives sit round their camp fires.

H

they had seated themselves, backs to the shed, and Lloyd was proceeding to mend a rent in the leather. She would call Johnnie, she decided, get him to mind the others. She hated the way he was for ever trailing after Lloyd. But what could you expect? A little fellow of seven loved to be out with the men, and the sooner a child learned to fend for himself in this country the better.

Her lips parted for a shout which congealed to a strangled intake of breath.

Once again round the corner came a figure, a painted buck.⋆ Red and yellow ochre and a white lime pattern on his body made him look like a walking skeleton. Quicker than thought the long shaft of the spear already quivering in his woomera † flew out. It missed the little boy by inches and buried itself still quivering, in the man's out-stretched arm. Before ever Lloyd yelled, the native was gone.

The woman ran across the hard earth, her tanned face livid, yellow. The child flew to meet her. The man lay picking at the spear hanging from his arm. His eyes twisted, terrified.

But there was nothing to see. Everything was silent, except for the short sobs of the boy and the cawing of the crows.

She left the four children with Lloyd in the front room while she went alone to the kitchen for hot water. Johnnie seemed calm enough now, only interested, like the others,

⋆ A male native painted in bright colours for corroboree ritual or fighting.

† A wooden instrument shaped rather like a long cricket bat with a hook at the end, used by natives in spear throwing.

in the barb stuck in Lloyd's arm, and keen to watch the blood oozing out. 'It was Billycan, that was,' the boy kept repeating excitedly. 'Why ever should old Billy do that?'

Lloyd said nothing. He was white and trembling. The woman, as she fetched the water, decided she would have to give him a little of the whisky she kept, hidden, just in case. Her eyes raked the plain and slid along the creek-bed. She wanted to keep her mind busy with observation, but there was nothing worth observing. Still only the silent countryside. She could sweep the horizon right round and see nothing. She found herself thinking that the gins wouldn't be coming up now—probably the camp was deserted; they had cleared to the hills. She couldn't expect John for another couple of days, either. Hastily she dragged her mind from such thoughts and ran back to the house.

She had already broken the shaft from the barb—only about a foot stuck out of Lloyd's arm now.

'It'll hurt,' she said to him. 'I'll have to cut it out.'

He whined.

'I'll give you something first,' she said and, going to the bedroom, came back with a tot in an old pannikin. 'There'll be another when it's over,' she said.

She sent the children away—told them to keep baby quiet; he was wide awake now and would begin fretting soon. Then she ripped up a sheet.

She hated touching the man. And he shrank beneath her gentle hands, whined again, begged more whisky. His beady dark eyes, set in a face dirty with half-grown beard, grew scared and shifty.

The woman said: 'It's got to be done, Lloyd. Don't be a fool.' And she did it. A bloody job. But at last it was finished, the wound bound, most of the mess cleared away. Lloyd had another tot. Then demanded the lot. Said he needed it.

'No,' she said.

'Yes, missus. You make no mistake about it. I'm having that whisky and then—well, I'm scooting.'

'Scooting?' she repeated blankly, her mind with the children.

'Scooting. Going. Clearing out. That's plain, ain't it? I'm not stopping here for no more blanky niggers to run spears through me! I'm off into the town, I am. The boss left one moke in the horse-yard, and that's mine. Or soon will be. I'm off. I'll tell 'em to hurry on out here, if you like.'

She flared. 'Thank you! Call yourself a man, do you?'

'Hell to you! I'm going. Anyway, you're all right, missus. The abos ain't got no call to touch you. Didn't you reckon they would all be gone?'

'Yes. But if it *was* all right, they would still be here. They mean trouble when they go.'

'Well, I tell you I'm not staying, anyhow.'

She noticed he was still trembling. 'Go, then,' she flung at him. 'You're no use as you are!' So that he would not discover her fear, she turned aside.

Too late she realized he was banging the door behind him and that the whisky bottle was under his arm. Like a fool she had let him take it!

She fought down her fears, and with a smiling face went in to the children. But Edie said, as she was pushed aside from the baby, 'Oh, Mum, how cold your hands are!'

Johnnie immediately wanted to go outside, but she forbade him. They had to stay and play quietly while she nursed the baby. And as she sat there, on the low chair her husband had made, her mind flew back and forth like one of the ever-hovering crows.

Presently the beat of a horse's hoofs hammered the silence.

'Mum,' cried Johnnie from the window, 'where's Lloyd going?'

'Just a message for me,' she answered tranquilly; but, sharp and bitter, her mind recalled the chance-heard remark of another man, an epithet applied to Lloyd. 'It's right, too,' she thought. '"Not got the pluck of a louse", he said. That's just what Lloyd is—vermin. No good in him.'

All the afternoon nothing stirred outside. The children grumbled at having to stay with their mother; they wanted to go down to the camp and play with the blacks. At sundown the woman fed them well, and put on what warm clothes they possessed. The nights grew cold outside. Then she made up a packet of food and filled three water-bags. She went into the bedroom, returned wearing a coat; in the secrecy of her pocket her fingers closed on the butt of a revolver her husband had given her when they first sailed north.

Already it had grown murky outside, with the swift falling of the Australian night.

'Come, children,' she said, 'we're going walkabout tonight. It will be fun to camp out in the spinifex.'

She could not repress a shudder. Often enough she had groaned over her rough little home. Yet how cosy it looked now, and safe! Filled with things she had herself fashioned from bits and ends, just to make it bright. She lit the lamp, set it on the table, and drew the curtains.

She picked up the baby. As she went out, followed by the children carrying the water-bags, she wondered if she was being a fool—subjecting them to unnecessary exposure. Well, in that case they could return in the morning. But she felt she couldn't risk the night; the natives might come after Lloyd again; they might come after the stores; that one act of violence might have gone to their heads. She did not want to think the childlike people she had so often looked after would set out to harm her children or herself; but she had to remember that two years ago they had not ever seen a white man.

She did not make the children walk far: if the worst befell they would have many miles to go. Just a little way on towards the distant settlement she took them; then, hiding snug behind an outcrop of rocks, she settled them down. Even though it was pitch-black by now, she knew that she was still within sight of the homestead.

Sam and Edie fell asleep. 'Mum,' whispered Johnnie, 'are you frightened of the abos? Don't be scared, Mum, I'll look after you. Why did old Billycan do that to Lloyd, Mum?'

'I'm not frightened,' she replied. How frightened she was! 'But I think they might go a bit mad tonight . . . Lloyd was a rough, bad man, son, that's why.'

An age she crouched there, it seemed to the woman. Even Johnnie prattled himself to sleep. She began to call herself a silly, nervous creature.

A tongue of flame leapt up in the darkness. To the

She could distinguish figures leaping like black imps in the blaze

woman it seemed to leap through her own veins. The shed! They had fired the shed!

Instantly with the light came sounds. The sharp, staccato barking of dogs, shrill native voices, yells, bursts of song. As the light gained she could distinguish figures leaping like black imps in the blaze of a second fire. That was the house! She knew now that the storeroom had been raided; she could see black naked figures posturing about, throwing things to each other.

The noise increased. She shook the children. Time to move. As long as the natives feasted and played with the fire she was safe; she still did not want to think they would hurt her—but they had burned her home. Guilty consciences wrought terrible crimes. They could track her so easily had they a mind.

She looked at the heavens, took a bearing south by the Cross and the cold sparkling Pointers, and stumbled off, the sleepy children dragging at her heels. There would be a moon later, she remembered with thankfulness, after Sam had been picked up and the place kissed five times— she had to take his water-bag, along with the baby, then. Yet she stumbled on, resolute, cheerful with the children.

At last the moon rose, but its fading brilliance only unleashed her long-held fear. The country lay spread about like a desert peopled with terror, a void filled by shadows having no substance. Cold, cruel, impersonal, rejecting the soft alien woman and her brood.

The baby wakened, began to kick and struggle. Her whispers and the thin cries of the children seemed to reverberate like the laugh echoing beneath a church dome.

She offered no comfort when Sam and Edie started to complain. She was sharp now. She gave the baby to Johnnie, and he staggered along as best he might, while the mother took Sam pick-a-back. She found the child's weight did nothing to deaden the nausea threatening to engulf her, the sickness of fear.

At length the keen edge of sensation dulled. She no longer looked at every shadow with a cold thrill of rigid expectancy; she no longer strained her ears for fancied footfalls.

She grew harsh with the children. A slave-driver. Even Johnnie sobbed at her rough words. And he was being so good! 'Don't fret, Mum,' he kept on saying. 'They wouldn't hurt us. Billycan's a mate of mine—they wouldn't hurt us.'

The night was without end; the country without end. Did there exist, anywhere in this grey and silver emptiness, human creatures other than black devils: were there houses, helping hands?

Dawn at last—and an unbearable radiance in the skies. A hard, rough land; and a sun gaining hourly in strength. A short sleep for the children. A drink of water and a piece of bread. Then up and on.

The woman felt safe from the natives now. She could reckon they would not attack until night fell again, if they were after her. That was what the men always said, anyhow. But if John were not already on the way out! The ghastly sickness swept back—they would all perish long before little legs could reach the settlement.

She was too tired to think for long. It took all her energy to watch. Up and on, then; up and on; through heat, with flies clinging and children crying. Hotter and hotter and hotter.

They had come on to the track—faint wheel-marks across the baked earth—soon after sunrise. It was Johnnie who spotted his father. The woman was trudging along with her eyes on the ground; she was carrying both Sam and the baby now. Breathing burnt her chest. Yet not until she looked into her husband's face did she realize *how* she must look. Haggard, livid, fallen-in, his face was. He had been riding, with two others, most of the night. That miserable Lloyd must have passed them, after all!

'Anna,' was all her husband could say for a bit. 'My God! Anna!'

The evil wrought by Lloyd was over, the woman told herself; but as she sobbed out her tale she knew it had only just begun. The other men were petting and soothing the children; Johnnie was boasting of all he'd done, telling them Billycan was a mate of his. Her husband's hand on her wrist felt safe, firm, tender.

'We'll take you into town, dearest,' he said. 'Then we'll come back and teach those black devils a lesson.'

'Lloyd!' she murmured.

'He'll have to leave the North, I reckon,' struck in one of the men.

'It was all his fault,' she repeated. But she knew it was no use arguing. The work of years had been destroyed; probably half their cattle had been speared now, too. What devils fear made of men, whether black or white—an hour ago she had been inhuman herself! But now, as she lifted heavy eyes to her husband's grim mask, she felt sorry for the natives.

TRAPPED

The author of this story was born in the Aran Islands, a group of three lying in Galway Bay, off the west coast of Ireland. These islands are noted for their high limestone cliffs, which fall steeply to the Atlantic Ocean, and for the rigours of bleakness and mist in which the islanders live. In certain parts the soil is so scarce that the villagers carry earth from crevices in the rocks and mix it with sea-weed to make gardens in which to grow barley and potatoes. It is against a background of towering cliffs and primitive poverty such as this that Bartly Hernon, the bird-catcher, lived.

NIGHT WAS falling. The sun was sinking into the sea, casting a great wide red arc of light over the calm water. The cliffs that had looked grey during the daytime were now black and their faces seemed to ooze water, a sort of perspiration that pours from them during the night. Beneath them the sea was a deep, deep blue, almost black, and the little waves never broke at all, but swelled in and out murmuring. It was very beautiful, silent and dreamy.

Bartly Hernon the bird-catcher had descended the cliff-path from the summit of the Clogher Mor and landed on the broad plateau that protrudes from the face of the cliff, about fifty feet above the level of the sea. To the left the cliffs curved inwards, forming a half-circle. They bellied out far over their concave bases. There were great wide clefts in them, like scars running horizontally between each

massive layer of stone that formed the foundation of the
earth above them. From the plateau the great height of
the cliffs made the fissures look small, but a man could
stand erect in some of them. And the little stones, that
could be seen wedged in their mouths here and there, were
really huge boulders, buttressing the upper layers of the
cliffs.

Hernon was a very big man with finely developed limbs
and a square muscular head. His face was tanned brown by
the elements and great strong fair hairs covered the backs
of his hands. He was all fairhaired and his face had the
gentle, passive expression of the man who never thinks of
anything but physical things. An ever-active, fearless man,
he was so used to the danger of climbing cliffs that he was
as surefooted as a goat. He carried a sack, a heavy short
stick and a small basket. The sack was to carry the birds.
The stick was used to club them. He stored the eggs in the
basket.

In order to reach the entrance to the lower fissure, one
he was to explore that night, he had to scale a very narrow
and difficult path along the cliff face for a distance of about
twenty yards. This path was formed by a portion of the
cliff coming loose and slanting out at an angle of ten degrees
or so from the cliff itself. It looked like a crazy structure of
boxes, piled one on top of the other irregularly. It seemed
that one had only to give it a slight push and it would
topple over into the sea. About five hundred tons of stone.
Between the cliff face and this slanting pile, loose rocks had
fallen. Along these rocks, Hernon had to go. He had been
many times through this pass and it had never occurred to
him that there was any danger in it. The broken pile had

been there as long as anyone in the district could remember. It had a name and it was part of the country. So it would always be there. If it fell it would be impossible to reach those fissures where the sea-birds lived, or, having reached them, to get back to the plateau. But among our peasants it was unmanly even to think of its being dangerous to go up that way.

Hernon took off his shoes and left them on the rock. He also took off his frieze waistcoat and left it with his shoes. He would leave them there until his return in the morning. He took a piece of the bread which he carried in a red handkerchief and ate it. The remainder he placed beside the waistcoat. If he got hungry during the night, very hungry, he could suck a raw rockbird's egg. It was very strong but very good to prevent that sort of hunger-sickness which men get sometimes in the cliffs; not from hunger but begotten of the terrific solitude and darkness of the caverns. The remainder of the bread he would eat in the morning, on his return, before climbing to the cliff-top.

He tightened his belt and began to climb. All those big rocks were loose and very smooth. He had to jump from one to another, gripping for footholds with his hands and toes, crouching like a dancer and then jumping, curled up in a ball, so that he landed on all fours. He got almost to the end of the pass when he missed his foothold. He swayed for a moment out over the sea. Then he gasped and swung himself in towards the cliff, grasping a pointed rock that projected. The rock held his weight until he reached another foothold in the entrance to the fissure. Then as he strained at it further to raise himself and thrust himself forward, it gave way with a rumbling noise. Terrified at finding the rock coming loose with his hands, he hurled himself forward on his face and clung to the wet floor of the fissure. He lay still.

It was the first time he had missed a foothold scaling that pass, and he was stupefied with terror. It always happens that way with a fearless man who has done daring things but has never met with an accident. He listened without looking behind him.

There was a dull rumble as the loosened rock fell with a thud against the slanting pile. Then there was silence for about half a second. Then the silence was broken by a slight snapping sound like the end of a dog's yawn. That sound changed into another and louder one, as of a soft mound bursting. Yet nothing seemed to move; until suddenly there was a tremendous crash. A cloud of dust rose in the air and the great pile of broken cliff hurtled down to the sea, casting rocks far out into the dark waters, where they fell with a pattering sound, while the bulk subsided to the base of the cliff and became still almost immediately. When the cloud of dust cleared away the face of the cliff was again smooth and unbroken. There was not a foothold for a cat from the fissure at whose entrance Hernon lay to the plateau beyond. It was a distance of twenty yards, past a hump in the cliff. Hernon was trapped.

He was perspiring. He turned his head and looked behind. When he saw the smooth face of the cliff, where a minute before there had been a pile of loose rocks and a path, his mouth opened wide and his look became fixed. 'Jesus, Mary and Joseph,' he said. Then he remained motionless for over a minute staring at the smooth, dark-grey bulging face of the cliff that cut off his return. He kept staring at it stupidly, as if expecting that the pile of rock would rise again and cover it. But the only thing that happened was that tiny rivulets of water oozed from it and began to descend slowly, dropping down to the sea, just like the rest of the cliff. It almost immediately looked old like the remainder of the cliff, as if it had been shaped that way for centuries.

'You horned devil,' muttered Hernon, suddenly becoming terrified of it and crawling away up the fissure on his hands and knees. The fissure was very low at its entrance. But it rapidly widened so that after ten yards or so, a man could walk in it, stooping slightly to avoid an occasional boss of stone that jutted down from the roof. Hernon, however, was so stupefied that he kept crawling long after he had passed the narrow strip, until he bumped his head against a boulder that propped up the roof. Then he jumped up and looked around him wildly.

Night had completely fallen within the caverns. It was pitch-black. But looking out to sea over the edge of the cliff, he could still see the water and the sky lit up by the twilight. He sat down on the rock to recover from his shock and plan some means of escape. But instead of concentrating on how he was to escape he kept remembering all the men in the district who had been killed in the cliffs: Brian Derrane, who fell from the top of a cliff while hunting a rabbit; John Halloran, who got entangled in a fishing-line he was swinging out and got carried out with it; and several others. Gradually he felt a curious longing to look out over the edge of the cliff and throw himself down.

He was not aware of the desire to throw himself down until he bent forward and looked down. It was about one

hundred feet to the sea. He could distinguish the forms of
large boulders in the tide and flat rocks with sea-weed
growing on them. And as he looked at them he felt a
sudden desire to hurl himself down. That terrified him.
He jumped up and crawled back, until he pressed his body
against the back of the cavern. He was quite helpless with
fear now.

He lay there for a long time quite motionless. It was
pitch-dark now. All sorts of sea-birds were flying in and
out. The whirring of their wings in the darkness was a
terrifying sound, because they were invisible and they did
not scream. They were all returning to their nesting-
places for the night, in the interminable holes in the fissure.
Hernon took no notice of this sound because he was used
to it. Afterwards, when the moon rose and the place was
lit up with a yellow light, he had intended to prowl among
the caverns and club the sleeping birds. But now he was
not thinking of the birds but of death.

It is extraordinary that physically fearless men like Hernon are always thrown into a panic like this when con-
fronted by something they cannot understand. They are
always eager to face danger when they can see it and understand its nature and touch it physically. But I have always
noticed among our peasants that these rough strong, un-
thinking men like Hernon are quite hopeless in a situation
that demands thought if they have no one to guide them.
Whereas the small, weak, cunning types of peasant, who
invariably avoid danger, are always subtle and resourceful
when placed in a dangerous position.

But very probably the danger of his position had been
discussed beforehand around the village firesides, as is the

custom on winter evenings, and he understood the hope-
lessness of it. It was absolutely impossible to reach the
summit of the cliff. It was two hundred feet away and it
bellied out, so that even if people came with a rope, the
rope would dangle twenty feet away from him, absolutely
out of reach. And it was equally impossible to throw a
rope from the sea, up a distance of one hundred feet.

At last the moon rose. Gradually the yellow light lit up
the sea, the cliffs and the caverns. It was very weird but it
revived Hernon. He was quite used to the moonlight in
the cliffs. It was something physical that he could understand. The birds were now all asleep and there was per-
fect silence.

He got up and began to walk along the edge of the precipice, looking down and examining its face, seeking a
path to descend. Even if he could get down to the sea he
would have to swim over a mile in the night before he
could get a landing-place, and there were sharks in the
water. But he could not wait till morning, until perhaps a
boat might come looking for him. He was too panic-
stricken to wait.

The fissure, in which he was, wound irregularly through
the face of the cliff for a distance of almost half a mile.
but here and there it was so narrow that there was only a
tiny ledge, a few inches wide, leading from one deep
cavern to another. These passages were very dangerous
even in broad daylight. But Hernon thought nothing of
them. He had stopped crawling now. He dashed along,
taking great bounds over pools, gripping the face of the
cliff and swinging himself out over the edge of the cliff to
reach another ledge. His figure, bending and bounding,

looked wonderfully agile and beautiful in the half-darkness of the pale yellow moonlight; the mysterious bounding figure of a cliff-man. He had dropped his basket, his club and his sack. He had lost his cap. His fair hair shimmered in the mysterious moonlight.

Although he had been panic-stricken when he was crouching under the cliffs, he was now perfectly composed physically. His limbs moved instinctively although somewhere in the back of his mind there was the picture of a skeleton that had once been found in these caverns. Some man, ages ago, had been wedged in among boulders at the back of a cavern and had died there, unable to extricate himself. That was a legend. It drove him on. But his body was cool and his limbs acted methodically, moving with supple ease, performing amazing feats of agility.

However, he went along several hundred yards without seeing the least sign of a path down to the sea. Then at last he turned a corner and came to a place called the Cormorants' Bed. Here there was an enormous cavern. Down from it to the sea there was a big black crack in the cliff. The cliff face was as smooth as elsewhere, but there was a long straight stone, pointed like a wedge, running straight down. Hernon looked at it and wondered could he grip it with his knees and slide down slowly. His forehead wrinkled and he shuddered thinking of it. He looked down. There were rocks at the bottom. He would be smashed to pieces if he lost his hold. Yet without pausing he moved towards the cavern. He rounded a very narrow ledge and stumbled into a pool at the entrance to the cavern. Immediately there was a wild screech and hundreds of great black figures whirred past his head, flapping

Hundreds of great black figures whirled past his head flapping their wings

their wings. He stooped to avoid them, because these birds, going past on the wing, could knock him over the edge of the precipice. Then when they had passed he groped his way to the wedge-shaped rock that ran down. He made the sign of the cross on his forehead, rubbed his palms together, grunted and stiffened himself. Then he gripped the rock savagely, swung his body around it and gripped with his knees. He hung on to it for a moment, like an animal crouched on its prey. Then he began to descend.

As soon as he moved downwards, he was seized with dizziness. His limbs shivered and he almost lost his hold. A prickly sensation went through his body to his heart, like a prod from a needle. But in an instant he stiffened himself and held his breath. The fit passed and he ceased to be conscious. His limbs moved mechanically and his eyes stared unseeingly at the wedge-shaped rock that he held. He went down and down inch by inch, each muscle rigid, moving with the slow, awkward movements of a bear, his broad back bent, his neck muscles cracking with the strain on his spine. His skin was perfectly dry, as if all the perspiration had been drained from the pores.

Then at last he found himself sitting on a rock at the bottom of the cliff. He still clung to the cliff, pawing at it, for several moments before he became aware that he had reached the bottom. When he did become aware of it he uttered a loud oath, 'You horned devil', and then perspiration stood out on his forehead once more.

But curiously enough, it was not through fear he was perspiring, but through pride. He had done a mighty thing. He had descended where no man ever had descended. Exalted with joy and pride, he waved his hand over his head and uttered a wild yell. The sound re-echoed again and again among the caverns of the cliffs, and before it had died thousands of sea-birds rushed from their ledges screaming. The air was full of terrifying sound. Hernon jumped from the rock where he still sat and, without pausing, plunged into the sea, terrified once more by the eerie sounds in the devilish caverns from which he had escaped.

The sea was dead calm, shimmering under the moonlight that fell on it, making a broad silver path with golden rims, while afar it faded into blackness under a starlit pale sky. On a level with the sea, the cliffs seemed to reach the sky. The sky appeared to be walled in by them, like water in a deep basin. Afar off on the left there was a sharp promontory where the cliffs ended. Beyond that there was a rocky beach below the village. That was where Hernon could land. It was over a mile.

He began to swim with all his strength, swimming on his side, heaving through the water with a rushing sound like a swan. He was a great swimmer. His beautiful muscular shoulders rose out of the water, his long arm shot out circularly, he thrust forward his other arm like a sword-thrust and then he heaved forward, churning with his feet, while he shook his head and spat the brine from his panting mouth. In the water he was conscious of no danger. All his muscles were in action and he saw the open sea before him to traverse. In spite of his terrific exertion in the cliff and descending, he was quite fresh and he never slackened speed until he passed the promontory. Then he turned over on his back and let himself be carried in by the great rolling waves that drive to the rocky beach. Then he turned once more on his chest and swam to the low weed-covered rock on which row-boats landed. He mounted the rock and waded on to dry land. He was safe. He rushed up the shore and knelt on the pebbles. Crossing himself, he began to pray aloud, thanking God. But while he prayed he kept thinking of what the village people would say of his heroic feat.

MY WHITE DONKEY

'WELL, BOYS,' said my father, 'no more talking now: time you went off to sleep.'

'Stay a bit, Father,' said my elder brother. 'It's so light: we can't go to sleep yet.'

I can remember now how very light the room looked. I can remember our two iron bedsteads, with the white counterpanes, and the bare stretch of uncarpeted boards: a spacious, airy bedroom for two boys of eight and eleven.

'Father,' said Goller—for that was my brother's nickname—'don't go for a moment. I must tell you. I must tell you. I took my new pony over that highest jump in the field, and he cleared it rippingly. And then he went at full gallop against old Thomas, absolutely whizzing: and he's every bit as fast. I swear he is. I'm going to call him "Demon".'

I kept silent. My mother appeared in the doorway to fetch father down to dinner.

'What Goller says is quite true,' mother said. 'That new pony is really fast, and he can jump, too. I think I made a good buy.'

'Father, he's ripping,' said Goller.

'And I'm going to hunt him. Aren't I, Mum?'

'We'll see,' said father.

'Of course I am,' said Goller. 'He's my pony. You can't stop me.'

'If you're going to talk in that silly way,' said father sharply, 'I shall certainly stop you.'

There was a brief, uncomfortable silence. Then Goller, trying to show that he did not care, made the remark that I had been dreading all the evening.

'I say, Father; *that thing*,' he said, pointing at me as I sat on my bed, 'is afraid of Demon. It's a funk. It's afraid of horses!'

I was scorched all over with shame, and felt my hands grow hot and wet. I could not look up and meet father's eyes: or mother's. I could feel that she was looking at me, now, with a kindly yet contemptuous smile round the corners of her mouth. She knew. Only an hour or two ago, she had watched the whole hateful scene, to which Goller was now referring.

'I can't,' I had said. 'I can't!' Then I had wept. And she, half smiling, half angry with me, as she was now, had said, in a spasm of irritation, 'What a scene! What a dreadful cry baby! All right, go in and play with your teddy bear.'

In the long silence that followed Goller's remark, I still knew they were looking at me. I felt as if I were alone before an audience of a thousand people, all staring at me in the light of our big, unfurnished bedroom.

'Shut up,' said father at length to Goller. 'Of course he's not afraid of horses.'

I was very grateful to father for coming to my rescue. I believed that somehow he would find a way to help me.

Mother and father went away, and I lay face downwards on my bed, with my pillow over my head, and refused to listen to Goller. His nickname was short for Goliath; father had called him Goliath when he was little more than a baby, because he was so unusually big and strong. Now Goller was nearly eleven, and I was eight.

For the last three years we had been living in London; then we had gone back to the country again. To Goller, riding and everything to do with riding was familiar: but in London, I had never learned to ride; I had never grown friendly with horses.

Now it seemed that mother and Goller did nothing but ride. Mother, looking unbelievably slim and boyish, seemed to be turning into a half-strange riding mistress. As for Goller he became bossy and aggressive. Horses brought out the most unpleasant streak in his character.

Meanwhile weeks had gone by, and it was not till Goller's new pony came that my dreadful secret was brought to light. I was afraid.

The next day, and the day after, no suggestion was made that I should go riding with the others. I tried to keep away from the rest of the family as much as possible. Father made no reference to the awful scene. I was constantly expecting him to talk about it: but he never did. One day, I was sitting on a window seat in the dining-room, more or less forgotten by my parents. Father had been reading news from the local paper to mother. He now turned to the advertisements and began to make comments on them; he was looking for horses, needless to say.

Suddenly he gave a laugh, and said to mother:

'Listen to this one, Ruth. "White donkey with a soft

furry coat, and very long furry ears; scarlet reins; used to children." Shall I get him?'

'What on earth for?' said mother.

'I dunno,' said father. 'I just wondered.'

'Don't be absurd,' said mother. 'Whatever use would he be?'

Father saw me looking round the edge of the curtains, and he went on reading another advertisement. I returned to my book, but I found myself picturing the donkey and thinking about him. Just how long would those ears be, I wondered; and would he be really and truly white.

A few days later father said to me:

'Want to come out in the pony-trap with me this morning; just you and me alone?'

'Ooh—yes,' I said. 'Where?'

'A little surprise,' he said.

So we set off, and after quite a long drive we came to a strange house; only the tops of three gables could be seen peering over a high stone wall.

'This is it,' said father. 'You wait here, and hold the reins.'

He vanished inside the wall, and presently came back with a stout, energetic lady, who said, 'So this is Michael, Captain Adams?'

'Yes,' said father. 'Come on, Michael. Shake hands with Mrs Davenport.'

We went through the house, and into the garden beyond, and into an orchard; and there was a small donkey, just as I had imagined him, snowy white, with ears so long that they fell forward as he cropped the grass.

'Talk to him, Michael,' said the strange lady. 'Pat him. He's used to boys: but mine are all too big for him now.'

Rather cautiously, I put out my hand, and patted the soft, warm fur on his neck. He took no notice, beyond twitching one of his long ears. His fur felt good, and I put my arm half round his neck. Slowly he raised his head, and, turning towards me, began in comical friendliness to rub his forehead up and down against my jersey: and then to nibble it.

I laughed.

'There,' said the stout lady. 'I told you he liked boys.'

'He's eating my jersey.'

She took a lump of sugar from her pocket.

'Give him this,' she said.

I gave him the sugar on the flat of my hand, and he put his ears back flat along his neck, baring his teeth and making a funny face while he took it.

We all laughed; and then I found his eyes were looking straight into mine. It was as if he had deliberately caught my eye. His eyes were large, soft as velvet, and a dark, almost a purple brown; they seemed to have a depth of humour, and a hint of reproach; as much as to say, 'Why laugh at me?'

'Well, Michael,' said father. 'Would you like to have him?'

'Me?' I said. 'How do you mean?'

'Have him for your own,' he said, 'as a pet; as a kind of extra large dog. Would you like him?'

'Yes,' I said.

'He's a very nice donkey,' said the stout lady. 'You'll find he has some very funny ways.'

A day or two later, father went off on his horse, and came back at a slow walk, leading Whitey. We put him in our orchard, and he stood quite still, deep in thought, and looking a little lost.

'He's feeling shy,' I thought. 'I must go and comfort him.'

So I went and put my arms round his neck, and he rubbed his forehead against my jersey. Then I fetched him a piece of sugar.

'Dear Whitey,' I said. 'Good Whitey. I hope you'll be happy.'

Father explained that Whitey was going to live in the orchard: he had never lived in a stable, and apparently did not mind the cold. We had a shed in one corner of the orchard, where we put some straw. Father said I was to keep an eye on the straw, and help to clean it out.

During the following days, I spent a good deal of time with Whitey. I rearranged his straw, though he had not slept on it. I took him some hay, though he preferred the long, fresh grass. I talked to him; and I felt that thoughts were passing between us, as I gazed into his solemn and darkly shining eyes, which I now saw were surrounded by long lashes. They seemed to be full of placid meaning, and in a way of advice. It seemed to me that he was saying, 'Michael, I'm afraid you are rather a silly little boy; but I like you all right, and I think we shall get on well together.'

And sometimes, he seemed to say:

'If you watch me, and take my advice, you will become less silly.'

That very evening his advice and his promise were put to a severe test. Goller, passing by and seeing me staring at Whitey in the orchard, thumped me on the behind and said, 'Hullo, a donkey looking at a donkey.'

I said nothing, but felt angry.

'I suppose you know why father's given you that silly old moke,' said Goller.

'Why?' I said.

He was nearly four years older than I was, and he had a crushing way of airing the fact that he was sometimes in our parents' inner councils.

'Do you really want to know?' said Goller.

'Yes.'

'It's because he despises you,' said Goller. 'It's a punishment. It's to make a fool of you. You aren't fit to have a pony, so you have to have a donkey. Gosh! Fancy being given a *donkey*!'

My heart beat, and a weak feeling came into my knees, at these words.

'No,' I said, 'that isn't true. That isn't what father meant.'

'Of course it's what he meant.'

'It isn't.'

'It is.'

'It isn't.'

'It is.'

'It isn't. It isn't.' My voice began to raise itself shrilly.

'All right,' said Goller. 'Why *did* he give you the donkey

then? Everyone knows it's your donkey. Father meant to show everybody what a fool you are. I know, because he told me. So shut up.'

Goller went. My inside self rushed round and round in a whirlpool of fear, of desperation, of shame, of renewed hope, then of further doubt.

Gradually I became less agitated. I found I was again leaning over the orchard fence looking at Whitey, as he grazed among the apple trees. I went into the orchard, and stroked him. Already I began to feel calmer. Then I put my arms round his neck, and said gently into one of his long, pink-lined ears, 'Whitey, is it true? It *isn't* true, *is* it?'

He raised his head from the grass, and shook it violently, and my heart bounded up with happiness. I suppose I knew vaguely that he had shaken his head because I had tickled his ear, yet it did not affect my happiness. I knew my doubts were unfounded. I saw that father, who had been so kind and gentle about the whole affair, could not possibly have played the cruel, elaborate joke on me that Goller had suggested. Goller's words were no more than a silly tease; and I had taken them seriously.

I clasped Whitey again, and he suddenly capered off round the orchard, shaking his head, bucking, kicking with his cream-coloured hooves, first to one side, then to the other. Then he walked slowly back and began gently butting me in the middle.

'There you are,' he said. 'You need never take so much notice of Goller again.'

During the next few days and weeks I enjoyed a good deal of Whitey's quiet and reassuring company. I came to know all his tricks and habits. I was always a little upset by the extreme loudness and the sudden onset of his brays, in which he seemed to be complaining that this noise should be his only tone of voice. I was also a little unhappy at a strange rolling trick. I only saw him do it once or twice, and then it seemed to me almost as if he did it in pain.

Soon, feeling a little bored with merely watching him, I almost unthinkingly scrambled on his back, helping myself by grasping handfuls of his long fur. He took no notice of me at all, but went on grazing and walking. I sat in a sort of hazy dream, feeling the warmth of his fur against my bare legs, and letting pictures and ideas flow through my mind. So we went slowly about the orchard. The next day we did the same thing again: and presently it grew into a fascinating game.

At first I merely wandered in thought, rather aimlessly, as we drifted round among the apple trees. Gradually, however, as day followed day, my imagination took shape. We began our journey by riding out of the orchard, and away through fields and woods. Then we began to climb, and we climbed for a very long way, rising high above the trees and woods on to the bare slopes of a huge mountain. It was a long journey, and we had to stop for meals in the forest glades.

At night we camped in a place very high up, and very still. The short mountain grass, the little scattered clumps of bilberry and heath were solemn in the deep light and shade. But the wonder of the scene was when we looked back. I still catch my breath at the memory. We seemed to see not so much a view, or a county, as half the world; with mountain ranges and cities and forests; with coastlines, and countries in the midst of oceans, and drifting cloudscapes.

We went on through high mountain passes, and at last came to a land where donkeys did not need to bray, because they talked. They shared the land with human beings: people and donkeys lived in happiness together; but on the whole, I should say, the donkeys were the superior race, and those positions in which wisdom and gravity were especially needed were occupied by donkeys.

Not all the donkeys, here, were on the same level of development. There were a large number that I came to think of as the crowd donkeys, the ordinary donkey people. These were all grey donkeys, such as you may see on our own fields, or on the sands; but they had more graceful shapes, silkier coats shading off into fine silver greys, or into blue roans; and all had the deep thoughtful eyes of the donkey race. A gentle harmony of peace rose from them, like waves of quiet music. There were, of course, a number of other sorts of donkeys: among them the beautiful white furry ones, like my own Whitey. I found to my joy that he was a prince among them; the white ones were all small and furry, and they added to the usual white donkey calm a certain sprightliness and humour. These donkeys were much honoured.

I spent so much time, weeks together, half a childhood, it seemed, in this land, that I could describe it at great length: its meadows, forest walks and cascades, its white villages. All the colours, all the forms in this country were more vivid and at the same time more softly luminous than colours and forms on the earth: as if everything were reflected in a pool of sunlit water. The prevailing mood was always one of peace.

Then came the crowning happiness, a realization that I and Whitey had a task to perform. We were 'bearers of good tidings'; and we had the power and the joy of carrying good news, to all the out-lying houses and hamlets of the country. How are such ideas put into one's head at the age of eight? I cannot say, except that I learnt them from Whitey.

Father had bought Whitey during the early summer: now the autumn passed into a damp, mild winter. Whitey remained in the orchard, living outside most of the time. It was only when the wind and the rain came from a certain direction that he took shelter in his shed. We tried him in the stable for a few nights, but he made it quite clear to everybody that he preferred his field.

One morning, when Whitey and I were together in the orchard, father came carrying a bit and the red reins, that had been described in the advertisement. I had never seen them before.

'I see you've more or less learned to ride Whitey by yourself,' he said, 'so I thought you'd like to have some reins.'

'Oh, thanks,' I said. 'Thanks awfully.'

I had never consciously realized, until this moment, that in the course of my imaginary wanderings with Whitey, I had in truth learnt to ride him. Barebacked, and holding on to handfuls of his fur, I had walked, trotted and cantered about the orchard. I had learnt to sit his funny little bucks and prances, and when I had fallen off his back into

K

the long grass, he had always waited and, in fact, invited me to remount.

So now I rode Whitey outside the orchard. I rode out with the other horses; though I must say Whitey always went best in his own little field. When the hounds met on the green of our village, I even rode with the rest of the family to the meet. Father was delighted. I was indifferent. I preferred my own private adventures with Whitey.

That day my brother Goller went on to the covert side with his pony Demon, and took part in a run. He came back simply stuffed with pride.

'Gosh!' he said to me that evening, 'you looked absolutely frightful on that moke of yours. Gosh, I was ashamed of being your brother.'

'I'd sooner be the sort of person that rides a donkey, than the sort of person who's always boasting,' I said.

'Little fool,' he said. 'No one who's any good at all ever rode on a donkey.'

'Yes, they did,' I said. 'Our Lord rode on a donkey coming into Jerusalem.'

For once Goller was completely floored, and the only answer he could find was, 'That's just about the sort of thing you *would* say.'

As a matter of fact I was rather shocked by my own answer. I had meant the resemblance to apply to Whitey, rather than to myself.

I went out into the garden, and through to the orchard. Whitey was, I thought, looking a little unhappy. He was standing with his knees slightly bent, his head drooping. Then as I approached him he fell, or threw himself, on to his side and began one of his strange rolling bouts. I watched, startled, and then suddenly frightened: because I realized this was not a game at all; it was a seizure, a fit of some kind. His eyes rolled up, his teeth were bared, in a nightmare grin.

The rolling went on, and he kicked violently in the air. In a few minutes the fit passed and he lay on his side panting and looking dreadfully limp. I sat down beside him, and after a while put his head on my lap.

'Whitey,' I whispered. 'My prince of donkeys. Do you feel very ill? Have you got a pain?'

He gave a long sigh, opened his eyes, and presently began to breathe more normally, but still limply lay on his side. 'Shall I cover him up with a rug?' I thought. 'Shall I find father or mother?'

I went to fetch father, and when we came back, Whitey was standing up again, but he was not cropping. He looked droopy and dejected.

'I don't think it was a fit,' said father. 'I don't think donkeys have them. Perhaps he's been getting attacks of colic. I think we'd better ask the vet to come along.'

'Colic? What's——?' but I checked the words on my lips. I could not bring myself to ask how serious it was. If the vet was coming, I thought, it must be bad.

However, the vet could not come the next day. I was unhappy and I watched Whitey all the time. That afternoon while I was alone with him he became very quiet and listless. I knew well enough that another attack was coming on him; and I believe he knew it too.

When it seized him, it was of increased violence. First

he trembled, as if a great hand had seized him. Then he fell on his side, and kicked spasmodically. His eyes rolled. He looked now as if he were possessed.

'Whitey! Whitey!' I cried out inwardly; though outwardly I watched dumbly and helplessly.

Then, as before, he rolled; he threw himself first to one side, then to the other: his cream-coloured hooves groped in the air, again and again.

The attack seemed to go on longer than I could endure: and before it was over, while these violent jerkings were still going on, he seemed to recover consciousness completely. He looked at me, and I saw clearly in his glance pain, fear, anxiety; yet, with it a look of self deprecation, of modest donkey apology, for the scene that was taking place.

Then he lay still and panting; terribly exhausted. I knelt down, and put his head on my knee. I hope he understood the meaning of my arm round his neck. As before, he breathed very deeply with a long sigh. Then all his limbs relaxed, and grew still. His water flowed from him, and I saw that he was dead.

It was some time before the family came back. I scarcely know how the time passed until they came. I was thinking of his last look into my face. Had he understood that my arms were round his neck? My passionate longing was that I should have helped him, given him some sense of comfort, of friendliness in his passing.

But what had he thought or felt? What soul was encased in that snowy body with its hideous voice and lustrous eyes now dead? What spirit had I met? What knowledge;

with its inner courtesy, its air of gentle disillusion; its acceptance of the world in silence, in wonder, and in humour. Oh, Whitey, Whitey. My prince; my modest prince of donkeys.

I did not cry. I could not cry for Whitey. He would not have cried.

Later, mother explained to me what colic was: but several days passed before father spoke to me about it again.

'I say, Michael, old man,' he said, putting a hand on my shoulder one morning. 'I am sorry about your poor old Whitey. We must find something else for you to ride. That's what we must do.'

'I want to ride Demon,' I said. 'I'm sure I can ride Demon now. I'm never going to feel afraid of horses again.'

'All right,' said my father. 'Good man. Come on, then: let's go and try right away.'

A NIGHT AT A COTTAGE

ON THE evening that I am considering I passed by some ten or twenty cosy barns and sheds without finding one to my liking: for Worcestershire lanes are devious and muddy, and it was nearly dark when I found an empty cottage set back from the road in a little bedraggled garden. There had been heavy rain earlier in the day, and the straggling fruit-trees still wept over it.

But the roof looked sound, there seemed no reason why it should not be fairly dry inside—as dry, at any rate, as I was likely to find anywhere.

I decided: and with a long look up the road, and a long look down the road, I drew an iron bar from the lining of my coat and forced the door, which was only held by a padlock and two staples. Inside, the darkness was damp and heavy: I struck a match, and with its haloed light I saw the black mouth of a passage somewhere ahead of me: and then it spluttered out. So I closed the door carefully, though I had little reason to fear passers-by at such a dismal hour in so remote a lane: and lighting another match, I crept down this passage to a little room at the far end, where the air was a bit clearer, for all that the window was boarded across. Moreover, there was a little rusted stove in this room: and thinking it too dark for any to see the smoke, I ripped up part of the wainscot with my knife, and soon was boiling my tea over a bright, small fire, and drying some of the day's rain out of my steamy clothes.

Presently I piled the stove with wood to its top bar, and setting my boots where they would best dry, I stretched my body out to sleep.

I cannot have slept very long, for when I woke the fire was still burning brightly. It is not easy to sleep for long together on the level boards of a floor, for the limbs grow numb, and any movement wakes. I turned over, and was about to go again to sleep when I was startled to hear steps in the passage. As I have said, the window was boarded, and there was no other door from the little room—no cupboard even—in which to hide. It occurred to me rather grimly that there was nothing to do but to sit up and face the music, and that would probably mean being haled back to Worcester Jail, which I had left two bare days before, and where, for various reasons, I had no anxiety to be seen again.

The stranger did not hurry himself, but presently walked slowly down the passage, attracted by the light of the fire: and when he came in he did not seem to notice me where I lay huddled in a corner, but walked straight over to the stove and warmed his hands at it. He was dripping wet; wetter than I should have thought it possible for a man to get, even on such a rainy night: and his clothes were old and worn. The water dripped from him on to the floor: he wore no hat, and the straight hair over his eyes dripped water that sizzled spitefully on the embers.

It occurred to me at once that he was no lawful citizen, but another wanderer like myself; a gentleman of the Road; so I gave him some sort of greeting, and we were presently in conversation. He complained much of the cold and the wet, and huddled himself over the fire, his teeth chattering and his face an ill white.

'No,' I said, 'it is no decent weather for the Road, this. But I wonder this cottage isn't more frequented, for it's a tidy little bit of a cottage.'

Outside the pale dead sunflowers and giant weeds stirred in the rain.

'Time was,' he answered, 'there wasn't a tighter little cot in the co-anty, nor a purtier garden. A regular little parlour, she was. But now no folk'll live in it, and there's very few tramps will stop here either.'

There were none of the rags and tins and broken food about that you find in a place where many beggars are used to stay.

'Why's that?' I asked.

He gave a very troubled sigh before answering.

'Gho-asts,' he said; 'gho-asts. Him that lived here. It is a mighty sad tale, and I'll not tell it you: but the upshot of it was that he drowned himself, down to the mill-pond. All slimy, he was, and floating, when they pulled him out of it. There are fo-aks have seen un floating on the pond, and fo-aks have seen un set round the corner of the school, waiting for his childer. Seems as if he had forgotten, like, how they were all gone dead, and the why he drowned hisself. But there are some say he walks up and down this cottage, up and down; like when the small-pox had 'em, and they couldn't sleep but if they heard his feet going up and down by their do-ars. Drownded hisself down to the pond, he did: and now he Walks.'

The stranger sighed again, and I could hear the water squelch in his boots as he moved himself.

'But it doesn't do for the like of us to get super-stitious,' I answered. 'It wouldn't do for us to get seeing ghosts, or many's the wet night we'd be lying in the road-way.'

'No,' he said; 'no, it wouldn't do at all. I never had belief in Walks myself.'

I laughed.

'Nor I that,' I said. 'I never see ghosts, whoever may.'

He looked at me again in his queer melancholy fashion.

'No,' he said. ''Spect you don't ever. Some folk do-an't. It's hard enough for poor fellows to have no money to their lodging, apart from gho-asts sceering them.'

'It's the coppers, not spooks, make me sleep uneasy,' said I. 'What with coppers, and meddlesome-minded folk, it isn't easy to get a night's rest nowadays.'

The water was still oozing from his clothes all about the floor, and a dank smell went up from him.

'God! man,' I cried, 'can't you *never* get dry?'

'Dry?' He made a little coughing laughter. 'Dry? I shan't never be dry . . . 'tisn't the likes of us that ever get dry, be it wet *or* fine, winter *or* summer. See that!'

He thrust his muddy hands up to the wrist in the fire, glowering over it fiercely and madly. But I caught up my two boots and ran crying out into the night.

BIOGRAPHICAL NOTES
ON SOME OF THE AUTHORS

T. O. BEACHCROFT was born in 1902. He was educated at Clifton College and at Oxford University, where
he gained a half-blue for running. He ran the half-mile for
Oxford in the relays against Cambridge in 1922, and ran
the mile in the Oxford–Cambridge Sports in 1924. He has
written many short stories, a number of which are about
young people. Some of the best of these are found in *A
Young Man in a Hurry*, *You must break out sometimes* and
The Parents left alone.

DORIS LESSING was born in 1919. She spent her childhood in central Africa on a farm which grew maize and
tobacco. For several seasons running, swarms of locusts
came down from the North—from Lower Egypt where
they breed—and settled on her father's land. Doris Lessing
has written many short stories with an African setting.
One of her best collections is called *This was the Old
Chief's Country*.

RAY BRADBURY is an American. He was born in
Waukegan, Illinois, in 1920. In his childhood he loved cir-
cuses and carnivals, and was fascinated by the mysterious
powers of magicians, conjurors and thought-readers. Very
early he wrote down the fantastic scenes and stories that
ran through his head. After High School he sold news-
papers on a Los Angeles street corner, and continued to

write one or two thousand words a day, most of which he burnt. On his twenty-first birthday he heard that one of his stories had been accepted for publication. Since then many of his stories have been published, and several have won prizes. In 1954 he wrote the screen play of *Moby Dick*. Among his science fiction publications are *The Golden Apples of the Sun*, *Fahrenheit 451* and *The Silver Locusts*.

NAOMI MITCHISON was born in 1897. She was educated at the Dragon School, Oxford, and at Oxford University. She married at the age of nineteen, and wrote her short story *The Hostages* when she was twenty. She says 'it was the first story I ever wrote, and I dreamt most of it'. Her gift of re-creating scenes from Greek and Roman life are revealed in many of her other stories and novels, for example, *Cloud Cuckoo Land* and *The Conquered*. The collection of short stories to which *The Hostages* gives its name is particularly well worth reading. The scenes of the stories range from the cities of the early Greeks to the castles and villages of Norman England. This long period of history is seen through the eyes of ordinary boys and girls.

KATHERINE MANSFIELD was born in New Zealand in 1888. Here she spent the first fifteen years of her life, and here she returned after three years of schooling in London to spend an unhappy and stormy two years before being allowed by her family to return to England. Her memories of New Zealand provided her with the material for some of her finest short stories. They were happy memories, because time and her lifelong habit of longing to be elsewhere than she was had spread enchantment over the scenes and characters of her childhood. Some of her best stories are found in *Bliss* and *The Garden Party*. She died in 1923.

FRANK O'CONNOR is the pen-name of Michael O'Donovan. This great short story writer was born in 1903 and went to school in Cork, Ireland, where, according to his own account, he received 'no education worth speaking of'. When he was quite young, however, he learned to speak Irish, and early came to love Gaelic poetry, music and legend. His deep knowledge of Ireland and his affection for his native countrymen are revealed in many of his short stories. Some of the best of these are to be found in *Traveller's Samples* and *The Stories of Frank O'Connor*.

HENRIETTA DRAKE-BROCKMAN was born in 1901. By the time she was twenty she was travelling with her husband in the north of Australia. This country was then still the land of pioneers, and conditions were not unlike those described in *Fear*. She met many natives who were seeing white men for the first time, and talked with settlers who in the past had had dangerous encounters with wild tribes. Many of her stories of Australian life are collected in *Sydney or the Bush*.

LIAM O'FLAHERTY was born in the Aran Islands, Ireland, where he spent the first twelve years of his life in great poverty. When there was no food in the house his mother 'would gather us about her at the empty hearth and weave fantastic stories about giants and fairies, or mime the comic adventures of our neighbours, until our hungry little bellies were sick with laughter'.* Liam O'Flaherty's best short stories are written about the neighbours of his childhood and about the animals and birds he watched as he roamed the island rocks and cliffs. *The Reaping Race*, *The Oar*, *Going into Exile* and *The Stolen Ass* are tales of Irish peasant life. *The Conger Eel*, *The Blackbird's Mate* and *His First Flight* show Liam O'Flaherty's love and observation of nature. All these stories are found in *The Short Stories of Liam O'Flaherty*.

RICHARD HUGHES was born in 1900 and was educated at Charterhouse and Oriel College, Oxford. Besides writing plays, poems and short stories, he is the author of two fine novels, *A High Wind in Jamaica* and *In Hazard*. The latter is a stirring story of the sea.

* From *Shame the Devil*, an Autobiography, by Liam O'Flaherty.